PERPLEXITY

BOOK ONE – THE PEPPERMAN MYSTERY SERIES

PERPLEXITY

BOOK ONE – THE PEPPERMAN MYSTERY SERIES

BILL BRISCOE

Copyright ©2017 by Bill Briscoe
All rights reserved.

No part of this book may be reproduced in any form or by any electronic or mechanical means, including information storage and retrieval systems without written permission from the author, except for the use of brief quotations in a book review.

This is a work of fiction. Names, characters, places, and incidents either are the product of the author's imagination or are used fictitiously. Any resemblance to actual persons, living or dead, events or locales is entirely coincidental.

Editor: Lori Freeland
Cover Design: Fiona Jayde, Fiona Jayde Media
Formatting: Tamara Cribley, The Deliberate Page

eBook ISBN: 978-0-9986425-2-9
Paperback ISBN: 978-0-9986425-3-6

http://www.billbriscoe.com

This book is dedicated to my daughters and their families — Blythe and Chloe Stenberg and Brook, Justin, and Foster Moore

CHAPTER 1

JIM

Cemeteries haunted my soul. Especially this one.

I parked my rental, a brand new 1987 Lincoln, on a patch of gravel under a low-hanging red oak and tapped a nervous finger on the steering wheel. A steel band wrapped my chest, smothering me. Suffocating me.

I walked a thin line of love and hate with Holy Cross Cemetery outside Belleville. I loved this small corner of New Jersey. For the last twenty years this well-manicured mound of grass had been the only place I felt connected to Dad. I hated it for the same reason.

But I needed to talk to him. Had to tell someone. Had to tell him.

I closed my eyes, wishing we were at the old house working on my pickup under a shade tree. That's when we'd had our best conversations. Wisdom was his strength. When I was seven and having problems with a street bully named Gerald, he told me to learn to get along or stand up for myself, leaving me to solve my own problems. But I was a long way from seven.

I latched onto the steering wheel so hard my hands quivered. What would he tell me now? Would the proud way he'd always looked at me change once he knew what I'd done?

Shaking off the heavy memories, I reached for the door handle and paused, my fingers trembling over exposing my dark secret. I slowly lifted the handle. The door cracked open and air rushed over my face, providing a brief calmness. I pushed against the door and stepped out, each stride toward Dad's marker cumbersome.

My heavy feet kicked up bits of dirt and grass. Invisible hands squeezed my heart.

I touched the top of the tombstone. "Dad, I miss your leadership and guidance, but most of all I miss you."

A few months after I'd turned seventeen, he'd fallen from an oil rig in Odessa, Texas. Overnight I went from all-state linebacker for my high school team to a stand-in father for my two younger sisters. Working toward the playoffs was overshadowed by working to help support my family.

Because my parents were raised in New Jersey, Mom wanted Dad buried there. She pulled me aside after his graveside service and told me we were moving to Belleville to be closer to her family.

I'd been stunned. All I could think about was my senior year. Not only had I lost my dad, my best friend, and my security, but moving would almost surely ruin any chance of getting a football scholarship to the University of Texas. And I needed a scholarship if I wanted to go to college.

A blast of cold air brought me back to the cemetery. A chill crept over my neck and vanished. A chill in the middle of July? Maybe it was an omen not to share my secret with Dad. What if he could hear me? What if somewhere, somehow he'd kept up with my life and all the things I shared here?

"Hey, Dad." I knelt close to the granite stone and ran my fingers over the etched letters. *Patrick Pepperman.* "Laura and the triplets are at Mom's. I wish you could see those little guys. You'd be so proud, and I'm sure they'd love their granddad. You could spoil them with ice cream just as you did me. We'll be heading home to Oklahoma tomorrow. My high school reunion was yesterday. Hard to believe it's been twenty years for the Class of 1967. I didn't recognize half the people. I'm sure they said the same thing about me."

I was putting off the real reason I was here. But, first, I needed to let him know I'd kept my promise.

A cloud slid in front of the sun, providing a temporary shade. I took a deep breath. Kept going. "Blythe and Brook came in for the weekend. You'd love being around your daughters. They're outstanding, vibrant people. Just as I promised you, I paid for their college and looked after Mom. She's steady as a rock, always putting others before herself. Still the same lady you married. And guess what? She's also a CPA. Worked hard to make that happen."

I twisted my wedding ring, glad Laura hadn't come. Things were strained between us lately, and the words I needed to say to Dad were hard enough to say in private. "Laura says I mumble in my sleep. Sometimes I wake up in the middle of the night because of nightmares. She knows something's wrong. The hurt look on her face begs for answers, but I won't tell her. I can't tell her. She'd never look at me the same again."

I stared at his marker, hesitant to go on. "I don't even know if I can tell you. But I have to tell somebody." My past hung over me like a heavy shadow.

"No one knows what I'm about to tell you. I've buried it too deep." I closed my eyes and let out a deep breath. "A couple of weeks ago I went to a stag party for a co-worker. Hadn't been to a bar in years." I opened my eyes and stared at the letters that made up Dad's name. "My friend is a biker on weekends, and the type of bar he chose, well, let's just say, not a place to take your wife. It was about midnight when a big bruiser poured a drink on a little guy's head. Déjà vu. Instant recall of a similar night in Minnesota.

It seemed as if the lining of my stomach was being peeled away like an onion. "Something happened years ago. I blocked it out for so long, but now it's back. Most nights I wake up shaking in a puddle of sweat."

I struggled to keep my gut from ripping apart. Perspiration soaked my collar. "It happened after a game when I played for the Pittsburgh Steelers. We lost to the Vikings on their home turf. Our charter plane had engine trouble, and the team had to spend the night."

Once the story started to inch out of my subconscious, the need to release my secret pushed me to finish. "After dinner, I left the team and went to a bar three or four blocks from the hotel. And drank too much, too fast." I'd never done that before. It was stupid. Irresponsible.

"A loud-mouth jerk pestered a little guy at the end of the bar. Even spat into the man's drink." It reminded me of being tormented by that older boy when I was seven. "I told the guy to back off. Someone called him Weasel. Appropriate, right? When he didn't back off, I slammed him against the wall, then the bartender got involved."

A single crow flew over Dad's headstone, screeching a hideous caw, bristling the hairs on my neck. Another cold blast of wind. An eerie stillness tingled across my skin.

I swallowed and licked my dry lips. "Weasel followed me out of the bar that night. Dad, he grabbed me from behind. And I lost it. I pulled him into the alley and beat him into a bloody mess. Wanted to stop." My voice cracked. "But I couldn't. I pounded and pounded until his nose exploded and blood gurgled from his lips. When he went slack on the wet asphalt, I ran."

My heart beat so hard I could hear it pounding in my ears. "The next morning the local news announced an unnamed man was found dead in an alley." I twisted away from Dad's tombstone. "I think it was him. I think I killed a man." Anguish mixed with relief flooded my chest.

A flock of black birds scattered from a grove of trees, squawking as though someone had forced their flight. A man dressed in jeans and a white t-shirt stood at the edge of the woods, legs spread, arms crossed.

My pulse quickened. I stood and our eyes locked.

He pointed at me, then turned and disappeared into the trees.

My gut screamed that something was wrong. Something pushed me, then a powerful shove as if someone had come up behind me. But there was no one. Just the urgency to move. Run. Get out of there.

I sprinted to the car. My fingers shook and the key missed the lock and dropped to the ground. I bent and grabbed it off the gravel road just as a bullet shattered the driver's side window, narrowly missing my shoulder.

My heart sputtered, then beat faster and faster. What do I do? Where do I go?

"Son, the keys... move now," a voice whispered. Dad's voice. "Move to the other side of the car."

CHAPTER 2

JIM

Dad's voice. How had I heard Dad?

I snatched the keys and scrambled around the front of the car to the passenger side, legs shaking like someone had beaten them with a rubber hose. Dizzy, I sucked in air and crouched behind the front wheel.

I eased my head above the hood of the car, just enough to see. Nothing there. Did the guy from the woods fire the shot? I opened the passenger door and scraped broken glass from the seat. A shard sliced into my left palm. The cut was deep, and blood snaked down my forearm. But I felt—nothing. I was numb.

Sliding over the seat on my stomach, I jammed the key in the ignition, started the car, then popped up and slammed the gearshift into drive. Checking the rearview mirror, I shot out of the cemetery, leaving clouds of dust from the graveled road behind me.

The torn flesh on my palm began to pulsate in pain, the numbness wearing off. I pressed the cut against my pant leg to stop the bleeding. Didn't work. My pants absorbed the blood.

Who would shoot at me? I pounded my left hand on the steering wheel. Pain reminded me of the wound.

Blood splattered onto the dash. Come on, Jim, think straight.

The police station. I needed to go to the police station and Chief Langdon, my mentor since high school.

Pulling up to the municipal building, I parked across the street and wrapped a handkerchief around my injured hand. My shirt and pants were stained red. My vision blurred as I walked into the station.

A female officer confronted me. "Sir, please stop."

I zombied past her.

"Paula, it's okay. I know this man." Chief Langdon ran toward me, his voice anything but composed. His silver, walrus mustache bristled as his arched lips exposed his coffee-stained teeth. He was so close I could see my reflection in his round, wire-rimmed glasses. "Jim, what happened to you?"

I struggled to speak through my tight, clenched jaw. "Someone just shot at me."

"Paula, get a towel. He's bleeding." He grabbed a chair and pushed it toward me. "Where were you?"

"Holy Cross Cemetery. Visiting Dad's gravesite." The soaked handkerchief dripped blood onto the linoleum floor leaving a circular pattern. Langdon was talking to me, but I was only picking up every other word.

Chief's hand moved to my shoulder and grounded me. "Did you see anyone?"

"Yes, a man in jeans and a white t-shirt, but I couldn't see his face. Too far away."

"Get patrol cars seven and eight to Holy Cross Cemetery, ASAP," Langdon shouted to the dispatcher, then turned to me. "Are you in town by yourself?"

"No, Laura and the boys are at Mom's."

"Call Laura. Tell her to take the kids to my house. I'll let Marilyn know they're coming."

I stood. "The shooter wouldn't go after my family, would he?"

He put a firm hand on my shoulder. "It's just a precaution. We have to play it safe. The attacker didn't get you. The next target could be them."

My stomach filled with acid. I was exhausted, mentally spent, as I reached for the phone on Chief Langdon's desk. My right hand shook so badly I had to steady it with my left. What would I say to my wife? All I could think was be calm, be calm, be calm.

"Where are you?" Laura answered. "The boys want you to take them for ice cream."

"I want you to get Mom and take the boys to Chief Langdon's house right now." I did my best not to frighten her. My voice was calm, message direct.

"What... why... what do you mean?" Her voice trembled. "Are you okay?"

My temper snapped. She just needed to be safe. "Just do it. I'm with Chief Langdon. Please, leave now."

"Okay... okay, I'll get the boys." She began to cry. "Whatever it is, be careful."

Chief looked at me, his expression was sober. "I'll need you to go with me to the spot where this happened. The sooner we get to the cemetery, the better chance we have to gather information while things are fresh on your mind. First we need to go to the emergency room to get your hand sewn up."

I nodded, but wondered if I could make it that far.

Walking to his patrol car, I became dizzy to the point of passing out. Chief Langdon opened the passenger door, and I fell onto the seat.

He bent over, eyes level with mine. "Do you know anyone who would want to harm you?"

I shook my head and wiped the sweat from my forehead. "No one." I'd wracked my brain trying to think who would want to kill me. I couldn't make sense of this.

Chief Langdon was quiet as he got into his side of the car. Maybe just as confused as I was. "What did you do this weekend? Anything I need to know about?" He drove us out of the parking lot.

I leaned forward to adjust the seat belt with my good hand. "Went to the class reunion… that's it.

"Who did you visit?"

"Everyone." I glanced at the towel wrapped around my lacerated hand. I wiggled my fingers. There didn't appear to be any nerve damage, but it throbbed, and the pain intensified. "But mostly Delmar Boldin."

"Any problems between you and him?"

"None at all. We've kept in touch since high school." Dizzy and nauseous again, it took all my willpower to keep my stomach from erupting.

Chief Langdon made a ticking sound with his mouth. "We may be overreacting a bit. We've had problems all summer keeping kids from hunting squirrels at the cemetery. This whole thing could be an accident. I'm not trying to downplay what happened, but someone could have made a mistake. Dang teenagers and their .22s. They've been a real pain in the rear."

I snapped my head toward the chief. "That may explain everything." But what about the guy in the woods?

"It could." His words were measured and his tone softened. "Let's not jump to conclusions. Someone wanting to kill you may be a stretch."

I wondered if he said that because he believed it, or because he wanted to ease my anxiety. Whatever his intentions, I relaxed. The entire incident could have been an accident… couldn't it?

CHAPTER 3

JIM

After a quick stop at the ER, expedited by Chief's orders, we approached the cemetery. My heart sputtered, then beat faster and faster as I looked to where my car had been parked. I pointed with my stitched, bandaged hand. "Pull up next to that big red oak."

I started to get out of the car, but I couldn't move — not from injury, but fear. Fighting my instinct to stay in the car, I forced the door open. With every step we took, I wanted to take two steps back.

Yellow crime scene tape flapped in the wind. Police personnel were checking the area for clues.

I thought about Dad's warning. Had it really been his voice I'd heard? I couldn't share that with Chief Langdon. He'd think I was insane.

The chief twisted one corner of his moustache. "The officers have marked this area for investigation." He removed his hat and wiped his forehead with the back of his hand. His voice measured and concise. "Can you go through with this?"

I nodded, but my shoulders slumped. The bits of broken glass and the police tape forced me to relive the nightmare. My body began to tremble. Not wanting Chief Langdon to see, I moved to the side away from him.

He either didn't notice or pretended not to. "Okay, which direction was your car facing?"

Pointing with my index finger, I made an imaginary semi-circle. "North. I entered from the gate off Ridge Road, then turned the car around."

He faced the gate entrance. "So, the front of the car was facing north when you parked? The direction we just came from."

"Yes." Scanning the landscape, hundreds of granite markers dotted the horizon. They looked like fish scales, lifeless and cold. My heart sank, thinking of Dad in this lonely abyss.

The Chief looked around. "With the information you're giving me, the shot had to come from the west. That big cluster of trees would be my guess, the ones about seventy-five to a hundred yards from here."

"The man I saw... he moved into that grove."

"What else can you tell me besides what he was wearing?"

"Big, but not as big as me."

Langdon placed his hands on his hips and leaned toward me. "Where's your dad buried?"

"Over there, about thirty yards from here." I was puzzled by his question. "What does Dad's grave have to do with this?"

"Sometimes people feed their anger by destroying property. It's a vindictive response. Let's go take a look."

He cautioned me to stay back from Dad's plot. "If there's any evidence here, I don't want it disturbed."

Chief Langdon examined the marker. "Everything looks normal to me."

"That's a good indication the shot was an accident. Right, Chief?" My words begged for validation.

He paused before speaking, looked down, then back up. "Could be. Very well could be."

When we returned to the station, I called Laura.

"Jim?" Her voice quivered when she answered.

"Everything's good." I tried to strangle my uneasiness.

"You don't sound good."

"I'll explain when I see you." I picked up a pencil and bounced the eraser on the desk. "Leave the boys with Marilyn. You and Mom meet me back at her house." I spoke softly, trying to put a positive spin on things. "I cut my hand on some glass, and I've got blood on my shirt and pants. Don't want the kids to see that. After I change, we'll pick them up and go for ice cream. This has been an unbelievable afternoon, but I think I overreacted to everything. Love you. See you soon." The words trickled off my tongue. Was I trying to convince her everything was okay — or trying to convince myself?

The man in the Minnesota alley flashed before me. I was taken back to the smell of wet pavement and me hitting him over and over. Could he be the shooter? How would he hunt me down after all these years?

The only good thing if it was him — I wasn't a killer.

CHAPTER 4

JIM

Chief Langdon dropped me off at Mom's house. I walked through the front door, knowing I couldn't reach the shower and clean up without Laura seeing me. My bloody shirt, pants, and bandaged hand made me look like I'd been in a street fight—and lost.

Mom sat silently on the couch, arms folded on her lap, body hunched forward, rocking.

Laura stood by the stairwell and quickly paced toward me with a hard stare. I could see fear packed into her glistening eyes as she focused on my blood-soaked clothes. Her arms trembled as she wrapped them around me. "Jim, are you all right? What's going on?"

I took a deep breath and slowly exhaled. "Hey, everything's fine. Mom, wish you had a bottle of Scotch. I could use a stiff belt right now." I patted Laura on the back and eased her away from my stained shirt. "Let me go take a shower. Then I'll explain everything."

Laura grabbed my arm and squeezed. She gave a not-so-subtle push to my six-four, two hundred-sixty-pound frame forcing me to step back. Her mouth clamped so hard her jaw shook. "You can't walk into this house looking like you've been wounded in a war zone and not explain."

"All right." I moved past the staircase toward the kitchen table, an arm around Laura's shoulders.

Mom pushed off the couch and came with us. "Laura, if it's okay with you, I'll open a bottle of Irish whiskey. Give Jim a little time to unwind and clean up."

Mom had whiskey? I'd never seen her drink more than a glass of wine. "Great idea. Laura, you good with that?"

She looked across the table at Mom and ran her hand through her dark brown hair. She nodded in agreement, but her tense body and icy glare said something different.

I went to the upstairs bathroom, turned on the shower, unbuttoned my shirt, then sat on the footstool to remove my shoes. The first sip of the hard liquor burned its way to my stomach. The second swig finished off the glass. The numbing effect relaxed my tired, tense body, but my left hand continued to throb. Maybe another whiskey would help.

I heard footsteps on the hardwood floor. Laura tapped on the door and walked in. "I have clean clothes for you. I'll leave them on the counter."

She shut the door and walked down the hall.

The cool shower ran over my head and took the edge off my day. The person who had stared me down at the cemetery looked more mature than some teenage boy hunting squirrels.

I needed to compose myself before going downstairs. Wished I had another drink. Or five. Explaining what happened at the cemetery, especially hearing Dad's voice wouldn't be easy. Maybe it would come to me. Maybe the whiskey would help.

I lumbered down the stairs, struggling to button my shirt. Mom and Laura waited in the living room.

"Let's go to the kitchen." The whiskey bottle was on the table. I poured another shot and eased it to my lips.

"Jim." Laura's words were stout and to the point. "I'm not waiting another second. Now get to it." She eased herself into the chair across from me, folding her arms on the table.

I knew it was time to cut the bull. I reached across and placed my hand on top of hers and gently clasped her fingers. "I went to Dad's grave today, just to be near him. I planned to stay only a few minutes because the boys wanted ice cream. The strangest thing happened. The temperature dropped, and the wind grew violent. The change was spooky, hard to explain."

I nervously circled my index finger on the top of the glass. "The wind calmed down, but the temperature plummeted again. The air was thick and muggy. I took the car key out of my pocket." I lifted my drink to stall—didn't want them to know about the person at the edge of the woods.

"Go on, Jim. What happened next?" Mom's demeanor changed making the question more of a demand.

"I dropped the key and reached down to get it. That's when a bullet shattered the driver's side window." I closed my eyes and gently rubbed my right temple.

Mom slapped the table.

Startled, I looked up.

"Jim Pepperman, you're not telling everything. What are you holding back?" Her head tilted forward, eyes fixed on me like a circling hawk.

Pressure mounted in my chest, and I bit my lower lip. "I didn't drop the key. It was ripped out of my hand." Total silence. A cold shiver flashed through me like a bolt of electricity.

Laura's faced went rigid. "You didn't tell us someone was with you. Who was it?"

I took another swig and set the glass in front of me. "No one was with me." It felt like my face was a picture book, stripped naked with nothing to hide. "Look, it's probably not what I thought. Chief Langdon said boys have been hunting squirrels in the cemetery all summer. He said the shot could have been an accident. It was an overreaction on my part. The darn fool kid wasn't paying attention to what he was doing. It's all a mistake. That's all it is."

Laura drummed her fingers on the table. "But you said the key was…"

"I think Dad ripped the key out of my hand and told me to run to the other side of the car. His voice was clear." I pushed my chair back from the table and stood.

Mom and Laura looked at me. Stone-faced. Then puzzled. Then shocked. They thought I was nuts. Especially Laura. She was a logical person and nothing I'd said made sense to her. It barely made sense to me.

It was as though all the air was sucked from the room before she spoke. "Jim, you've been under lots of pressure today. I have to get the kids from Marilyn. When I get back, we'll take them for ice cream. Then we'll talk about all of this tonight." Laura reached down and stroked my head, then kissed me on the cheek. Her words were comforting, but I knew she didn't believe the part about Dad.

After Laura left, Mom sat back down at the table. "Jim, you've always gone to your dad's gravesite. What do you do when you go there?" The inflection in her voice indicated she wanted to tell me something.

My legs were nervously pumping up and down under the table. It was time to level with her. "Do you remember the day I went to the site where Dad died in Odessa?"

"Yes. Spring of 1967. The day before we left Texas. It was raining so hard I begged you not to go." Mom relived the dark days of our family's tragedy in a sad, monotone voice.

"That's right. It was something I had to do, something compelling. Can't explain it. Kneeling on the spot where Dad fell, I made a promise to take care of you, Blythe, and Brook. At seventeen, how could I do it… be a provider? I worked summers and weekends during football season because of that promise."

I picked at the bandage on my hand to gather my thoughts. "The cemetery is my refuge—the place I go to let Dad know how the family is doing. Today I told him the promise had been fulfilled. Blythe and Brook graduated from college and are fantastic young women. Mom, you're doing great. It wasn't easy. I should have told you about the promise, but it was a man-up thing between Dad and me."

A quick glance out the kitchen window showed a gentle breeze moving through the trees. That gave me a warm, comfortable feeling, not like the popping, twisting branches at the cemetery. Turning to face Mom, I placed my hand on her cheek. "Dad's voice was real. It happened."

"I believe you Jim." A tear ran down her cheek. "You see, I've heard his voice, too."

"When did Dad speak to you?"

"That night when you went to the place where he died. Flash flood warnings were issued and people were advised to stay off the roads." Mom brushed away a single tear as she continued. "I was so afraid something would happen to you. I went to my bedroom and prayed for your safety. A bolt of lightning knocked out the power, and I was alone in the dark. I'd never felt so helpless."

She touched her lips with the tips of her fingers. "Another bolt of lightning struck a tree in the backyard. It sounded like thousands of firecrackers were set off at the same time. Then it happened.... Something appeared in front of me by the closet. It was bright, but a fuzzy bright. I could see the outline of a man. Then he spoke." Mom went silent, body rigid. The one tear turned into many. She was crying, but it was a silent cry.

"Go on Mom. What happened?"

She turned her head to face me. "Your dad said, 'Liz, don't worry. I'll protect Jim. He'll be safe.' After he spoke I had a peaceful serenity that is almost impossible to describe. It was as if I had died and my body was levitating, upward toward heaven. Then the silhouette disappeared. It was over."

'Did Dad ever come to you again after that night?"

"No, and because of that, I felt hearing him never happened, just something I imagined, but now you've heard him too."

Mom wiped the tears from her face with the palm of her hand. Her shoulders, once tense, seemed to relax. I supposed she was relieved that someone else had heard Dad's voice. We sat next to each other without speaking for what seemed an eternity.

Then I turned to Mom. "This needs to be our secret. No one must ever know what we experienced."

Her mouth pursed as she heard what I said. "The only positive thing coming out of this ordeal is you hearing your dad, too."

I nodded.

CHAPTER 5

JIM

I waited on the porch of Mom's house for my two-year-old triplets, Ronnie, Leon, and Chuck. I couldn't think of a time when I wanted to see my kids more than now. Today's challenges had put life in perspective.

Laura parked the car and helped each of the little cubs out of his car seat. Noticing me on the front door steps, the boys shouted, "Ice cream, Daddy, ice cream."

Ronnie saw my bandaged hand first, pointing toward it. "Hurt hand? Daddy cry?"

I nestled all three. "No, Daddy didn't cry." I looked at Laura. She had a smile that would stop a train. Thinking about my kids not having a daddy was more than I could take. I shook that thought from my rattled mind — too painful and too sad.

Chuck looked at Laura, stuck out his hand, and moved his fingers. "My hand hurt. Want Band-Aid like Daddy."

Now all three wanted their hands wrapped. Laura bent down and placed her hands on her knees. "Well, we better get those boo-boos fixed. Let's go find some Band-Aids."

The boys slipped out of my grasp like lard on a hot griddle.

I didn't know if they were more excited about the ice cream or getting their hands bandaged. I stayed on the porch and watched as they scampered down the hall leading to the kitchen, asking for their Mema.

Telling Mom and Laura about the cemetery and hearing Dad's voice was difficult. I knew Laura would question Dad's whisper. How could I explain to her what I didn't understand myself? One thing was certain — the man in the alley in Minnesota would remain a secret.

God help me if they ever found out.

CHAPTER 6

JIM

The fan above the bed made a soft, whispering sound as it pushed the cool air toward my sweating face. The beads of perspiration were caused by nerves, not the heat of a hot summer night. I hated it when I smelled my own sweat.

My mind twisted things. I could answer questions about the shooting, but questions about Dad's voice — what would I say to convince Laura? I could tell her maybe I'd been wrong. Maybe I hadn't heard him. No, I couldn't. Dad's words were clear.

Motionless on the bed, I stared at the ceiling, licking my dry lips. I heard a door open. Laura switched off the bathroom light. Utter darkness, except for the street light partially blocked by a tree branch. I could see Laura's silhouette easing into the bed as she turned on her side away from me.

There was a crushing vacuum of silence. A good five minutes passed. "Jim, is there something you need to tell me about your past?"

Did she know about the man in Minnesota? How could she?

"What do you mean?" I sat up. My tone was elevated and direct.

She turned, facing me. "Have you made enemies? Did you get threats when you played for Pittsburgh? You know how fanatical fans can be."

I relaxed. She didn't know my dark secret. "I can't think of a single person that had it in for me. I've thought about this over and over. It has to be a kid with a .22 who made a mistake. I honestly believe that." Not sure what I just said, but wanted to reassure Laura.

I could see enough of Laura's face to know she was trying to smile, but she seemed overpowered by confusion and uncertainty. She grabbed my arm and moved close to me. "Really, do you think that's it?"

"Absolutely. I overreacted. Sorry for putting you through this. No one wants to kill me. Even Chief Langdon thinks it was an accident."

Laura tilted her head back. "Just you saying that makes me feel better." She paused, then continued. "About hearing your dad. Could it be you thought you heard him?" She twisted the covers. "Being at the cemetery... the strange weather... could you have imagined hearing him?"

I was relieved, knowing this was my way out—for now. "I think you're right. Let's keep this a secret between you, Mom and me. Boy, what a day. Glad we're going back to Oklahoma tomorrow. We'd better get some sleep. We'll talk more about this when we get home."

Her body seemed to relax. She kissed my cheek and turned on her side, away from me again.

My eyes were wide open as I stared out the window, but all I was seeing was the cemetery, and hearing Dad. I did hear him. It happened.

Setting the departure time so early in the morning was a dumb move on my part. Laura reminded me of that as I stepped into the shower. Taking extra precautions to keep the bandage out of the water was no small task in the tiny stall.

The wall clock in the bathroom caught my attention. "Laura, I'll get the boys dressed. We're running late." Because they hadn't eaten, the triplets were wilder than a pack of gerbils. For a change, getting the triplets dressed was easy. I took them down the stairs. Mema was ready for them in the kitchen.

Mom chuckled as she fed the boys. Some of my fondest memories occurred watching them eat. Although very similar in many ways, each had his own style of eating. Leon was a bit of a neat freak. He would take one bite of food at a time using his spoon. Chuck cared more about drinking his milk or juice than the meal. Ronnie—the messy one. Spoons were a nuisance. He went full-bore, fingers only.

The morning was hectic, but with Mom driving us we managed to get to the airport on time. Laura and the kids said good-bye to her while I unloaded the luggage and put it into a rental cart. The smaller bags kept falling off.

I was the last to give Mom a hug. Her smile was a plaster smile, and the hollow look in her eyes broke my heart.

She pulled herself close to me and whispered, "I'm glad we talked about your dad."

I gave her a squeeze and kissed her on the cheek. "Everything's okay, Mom. Don't worry about the shooting. It was an accident."

It took us fifteen minutes to get from the terminal to our concourse. Thank goodness for pre-boarding. Once we loaded onto the plane, Laura took Ronnie and Leon and sat across the aisle from Chuck and me.

The engines revved up, preparing to depart. Then they were powered back. The pilot came out of the cockpit and talked to one of the flight attendants.

I looked at Laura. "Bet there's something wrong with the plane." She closed her eyes and puffed her cheeks.

The attendant approached me. "Are you Mr. Pepperman?"

"Yes."

"Would you come with me please?"

I looked at Laura as I unbuckled my seat belt. "Probably left one of the carry-ons in the waiting area."

Laura stood and opened the overhead bin. "Where is the B-A-G with the C-O-O-K-I-E-S?"

I gave her a love pat on the top of her head and grinned. "Laura, you don't have to spell bag, but the B-A-G is in your seat."

She stuck out the tip of her tongue.

The flight attendant escorted me through the plane's gateway. I expected to see an airline staffer holding one of our tote bags. I scanned the area, but no employee with our lost item.

Someone tapped me on the shoulder. It was Chief Langdon.

CHAPTER 7

JIM

My heart flash-froze when I saw Chief Langdon and those drooped eyelids. "Go back on the plane and tell Laura there are some loose ends I need to tie up with your case." His tone was soft, yet firm. "Explain that you'll be home in a couple of days. Do your best not to frighten her."

My stomach knotted as though someone punched me. "What is it?" I asked the question, not wanting to know the answer.

Langdon gave me a cold stare and nodded toward the plane. "Go tell her now. Then we'll talk."

When I got back on the plane, Laura was in her seat fumbling through a travel bag. She looked up. Our eyes locked.

I shook my head and gave her one of those fake smiles that forced the corners of my mouth to turn upward. "Honey, Chief Langdon needs me here to follow up on a few things. I want you to go on home, and I'll come in a few days."

My wife was not a person to conceal her feelings. She struggled to unbuckle her seatbelt. "Jim, we'll stay with you. Come on boys. Let's go with Daddy."

Resting my hand on the overhead bin, I leaned forward. "No, Laura. It's just a few days. I'll call Brenda and Mike to meet you at the airport and help with the boys."

She blew a wisp of brown hair from her cheekbone and cut her eyes up at me with a you're-not-telling-me-everything look. "Call me tonight and explain why you're staying."

I nodded, smiled and touched her face. "Okay, that's fair. Boys, take care of Mommy, and be good."

My sons reached for me and began to cry. Hugging each of them, I left.

A sickening tingle wrapped around my heart. Langdon pulling me off the plane was serious, but how serious?

We went to the Belleville Police station. Chief Langdon unfolded his arms, paused, then pulled a plastic bag from his drawer. "Here's what I was talking about." He rested his elbows on the desk.

My anxiety level spiked.

"This was under the station door this morning." His voice stayed flat. "Addressed to me." He pushed it across the desk.

I picked at my upper lip with my thumb and index finger, afraid to see what was inside. I held up the clear bag that encased the note spelled out with red plastic stick-on letters.

The first bullet missed Pepperman's head.

The next, you'll find him dead.

My hand shook as I stared at the threat. My breath rushed out of me. I raised my head and managed a weak reply. "Do you have any clues as to who's after me?" My heart pounded against my rib cage. I prayed for a simple answer, some prankster with a warped personality who'd picked me at random. Hope flickered for a moment, then evaporated.

Chief Langdon leaned back in his chair. "We've checked for prints. There's nothing. Now, once again, who do you think wants you dead?"

"I have no idea." I clenched and unclenched my fist.

He stood up and pounded the desk. His eyes bored into me. "Come on, Jim. This is serious."

I shook my head.

"What about the guy in high school that bullied you? The good football player who was kicked off the team?"

"Phil Anderson? That was years ago. I haven't seen him since graduation. After high school we never spoke again."

Chief Langdon took off his glasses, tossed them on his desk, and rubbed the bridge of his nose. "Okay, okay. I'm still going to consider him a suspect. What about college or the years you played with the Steelers? Anybody?"

I paused. "There was one player in Pittsburgh who hated me. He was starting linebacker until he sprained his ankle. I took his place. He never got his job back."

Chief put his glasses back on and flipped the pages of his tablet. "What's his name?"

"Darren Colby."

"You know where he lives?"

"No... uh, maybe Denver. That was the last team he played for."

"Tell me about him."

"A loner. Never got along with anyone. After his ankle healed and he returned to practice, he cheap-shotted me several times in drills. Once, he clipped me from behind, a nasty cut-block. The team and coaches had to separate us." I rubbed my right knee, the knee that received the brunt of his stupidity.

"Go on."

"Went on all year. It got so bad Coach Charles dismissed him from the squad. Not just because of me. He was sour, a negative influence on the whole team."

"Jim, you've got a history of getting players kicked off your teams." He twirled his pen between his fingers. "Can you think of anyone else who could be holding a grudge?"

I hesitated, then nodded. "Laura."

Chief Langdon's head popped up. "Laura? What the heck are you talking about?"

"Maybe this is about her. She was engaged to a doctor in Philadelphia. She broke it off to marry me. A real hot head. He lost it, even threatened her. Laura said he pushed her around and called her names."

"Who is this guy?"

"Dr. Neal Sullivan."

Chief continued. "How well do you know him?"

"I don't. Only met him once."

Langdon placed one hand over his mouth. "Jim, the guy who wrote this note shows signs of being a real nut job." It seemed he wanted to muffle the bad news. "The fact that he sent it to me indicates this creep appears cocky — extremely confident and smart. My gut tells me this is real."

CHAPTER 8

JIM

Chief Langdon's office seemed to be my home away from home. I'd been here so much my favorite chair had become my best friend.

"Jim, the Belleville Police Department works closely with the Newark station. I've asked a detective from there to meet with us. His name is Sean Halpin, a retired Air Force colonel. Sean's highly decorated — served with the Air Force's Office of Special Investigation. He's been in the private sector for over ten years. I called him as soon as I got the note. Halpin's the one who wanted you off the plane."

Out the window, I saw a new black Ford pull into the parking lot. A man in a dark suit, white shirt, and red tie stepped out, his gait powerful and authoritative. Langdon didn't have to tell me who it was. His appearance demanded respect. The tall, fit man stepped into the office. His black hair had a dusting of gray, cut short with military correctness. His shoes were polished to perfection.

"Jim, this is Detective Sean Halpin." The Chief introduced us.

The handshake was firm, but not overpowering. The heavy bass in his voice added to his presence. "Please have a seat, Mr. Pepperman. I'm sorry I had to ask you to stay, but it's important I get some initial information directly from you." He motioned to a chair and got right to the point.

This guy was a no-nonsense person. That impressed me. I was ready to answer his questions. "Let's get to the bottom of this. The sooner the better."

Detective Halpin squared his chair in front of me, crossed his legs, placed his fingertips together. "You played football for the Pittsburgh Steelers. I'm certainly a fan of yours and the Steelers. The 1972 playoff game against Oakland... what's the name of the running back who caught the deflected pass and scored with seconds left on the clock?"

"Harper, Franco Harper."

"Yeah, that's it. Greatest game ever."

"What's your job now, Mr. Pepperman?"

"Civil engineer for Phillips Petroleum."

I appreciated the detective breaking the tension with small talk. It had a way of bonding the two of us.

Detective Halpin walked over to the coffee pot. I couldn't help but grin when he straightened the coffee mugs, the sugar jar, and the stirring straws after he filled his cup. "I understand you live in Oklahoma. Why were you in Belleville over the weekend?"

"My twentieth high school reunion."

Halpin nodded, then smiled. "Ah, yes, interesting times. Bet you had some surprises when you saw your classmates."

I eased back in my chair. "Most definitely."

Halpin took a sip, then set his mug on Langdon's desk. "Chief Langdon told me you had some problems in high school with a classmate. What's his name?"

"Phil Anderson." I glanced at Langdon. Then back at Halpin. "Look, the problems we had were kid's stuff. I haven't seen him since graduation."

The detective pushed out his lower lip, then angled his head. "What kind of kid's stuff?"

"He had a crush on Laura. She's now my wife."

"Did you two get in a fight over her?"

"No, she went out with him one time. But… one day after football practice he challenged me to a fight. We went to the park with the whole team following us. I humiliated him in front of our peers. It wasn't pretty."

"Why did he challenge you?"

"Bad blood. He was captain of the football team and looked at me as a threat to his leadership."

Halpin reached for his coffee and took another swallow. "How were you a threat?"

"I guess the players looked up to me. Coaches too. Phil accused me of getting him kicked off the team, but it wasn't me. It was his attitude. Everyone knew that. After I signed a football scholarship with OU, he came after me with a baseball bat one night after work. He was jealous."

"Was he at the reunion?"

I shook my head. "No."

"Okay, let's get back to Sunday when you parked at the cemetery. Was the driver's side window rolled down?"

"I cracked it when I parked. I didn't want the car to heat up."

"And the passenger side window, was it cracked too?"

"No, I rolled it all the way down."

Halpin made a fist and gently tapped his lips. "Why did you roll the passenger window all the way down? I would think you would only crack it like the driver's side."

"The glass was tinted, and there's a certain headstone that helps me locate Dad's gravesite. I rolled the window all the way down to find it."

"So the bullet shattered the driver's side window and exited through the open window on the passenger side?" He jotted a note in his small hand held tablet.

Chief Langdon spoke up. "That's what we think."

Detective Halpin tapped his fingers on the arms of the chair. "Let's go to the gravesite. You okay with that, Chief?"

"Sure, we have the Crime Scene Investigation crew out there now looking for evidence."

At the cemetery, Chief Langdon went to the CSI team. I stood under a large red oak and watched Halpin. He took off his sunglasses and scanned the area. Although I'd just met the Newark detective, I was glad he was working my case. He appeared to be thorough, a take-charge guy.

Suddenly my pulse quickened, sweat popped out on my forehead. A slow electric current seemed to pull up my backbone. My mind flashed back to the sound of the glass breaking, the smell of blood. Fear clutched me as if the shooting was happening all over again. I had to get out of there.

Halpin approached me as I was about to bolt. "Jim, the CSI will work day and night until they finish. They won't leave the scene until they're satisfied that nothing else can be done. Let's go back to the police station. I have a few more questions."

As we walked back to the car, Halpin stopped me and looked me straight in the eye, "Oh, one more thing. Do you always go to your dad's grave when you come home?"

"Yes, but why that question?"

"Someone could know that about you and set up the shot."

Halpin took a handkerchief out of his pocket, cleaned his sunglasses, held them up to check for spots, then stared at me, a hard stare. "Why do you go?"

"It gives me peace of mind."

He nodded, put the handkerchief back into his pocket, and slid the shades onto his face. "When we get back to the station, I want you to fill me in on this Anderson fellow. You can make arrangements to go home tomorrow. I know your family's anxious. We'll keep you posted on the evidence. And, Jim, Chief Langdon does have all your contact information, right?"

"Of course."

CHAPTER 9

JIM

I didn't call Mom to let her know I was pulled off the plane. What needed to be said couldn't be explained over the phone. I pulled into the driveway in a rental car.

She was watering her flower bed. She gave me a side-eye and dropped the hose.

I had a pretty good idea what was on her mind.

Her head dropped. She knew something was wrong. The look on her face, the sad eyes, and slumped shoulders spoke volumes. She removed her gardening gloves after she turned off the faucet. She tried to smile, but confusion swirled in her expression. It was one of those forced smiles, a cover-up smile. "What happened?"

"I told Laura to go back to Bartlesville. I had to stay one more day for your world famous crab cakes."

She angled her head and gave me a look that said I was lying. "Come on in. You must have a lot to tell me." I followed her into the kitchen. "You want something to drink?"

"No, but we do need to talk. Let's get this over with." I walked back and sat on the sofa. My right foot tapped nervously on the hardwood floor.

She was drying her hands on an embroidered cup towel as she entered the living room and eased into her recliner, crossing one foot over the other.

"Chief Langdon asked me to stay in Belleville because someone wrote a note, a death threat meant for me."

Mom sucked in air as she closed her eyes. "Who, Jim? Who would want to harm you? Why? Tell me."

"I swear, I've gone over everything. I can't think of a single person... no one."

"I can't believe this is happening. This is the sort of thing you see in movies, but not to our family. Could it be a mistake?"

I leaned forward, rested my elbows on my knees, and clasp my hands. "I suppose it could be someone playing a sick joke, but we have to look at it as though someone really means it."

"How are you going to deal with this? How are we going to get through this?"

There was a silence that roared in me. "The only thing we can do is believe in the police. And, I have to be very, very cautious. I know my being here puts you in danger, but I don't know where to go."

Mom gave me one of those motherly smiles that only a mother can give. "Don't worry about me. I can take care of myself."

All of the events of the past few days rolled toward me like an approaching storm. There was a sharp, cold tearing in my stomach. My sixth sense told me I was going to be tested, tested beyond anything in my life.

Suddenly, a measure of calm returned. The abject fear that had consumed me passed. My breathing slowed.

A deepening warmth permeated my body, and I knew where I would put my trust. In God. He was in charge of my life.

After dinner Mom and I sat on the front porch in her paint-worn Adirondacks. Watching the neighbors drive by on their way home from work made me realize I took routine problems for granted. Oh, for those days to return.

CHAPTER 10

JIM

THERE WAS NOTHING I'D DONE TO MERIT SOMEONE WANTING to kill me. The shooter had to be a sicko. Guess you could make that point about anyone driven to murder. The possibility existed that whoever wanted me dead might succeed. But, the deranged idiot who wrote the death threat didn't know how I was wired.

Even though I had been home only a day, the family routine returned to normal. We'd just finished supper, and Laura was trying to get the boys cleaned up and ready for bed. How could the triplets be so different? Ronnie hated baths. Leon loved them, and Chuck, he thought the tub was one big potty. Couldn't put him in there with the other two.

"Jim, help." Laura, in her usual panicked voice at this time of night, hollered at me. "Ronnie's buck naked and just ran out of the bathroom. Leon's in the tub. Chuck just climbed in and is peeing."

I was drying dishes and busted out laughing. Laura didn't sound amused. Her cries of frustration confirmed my point. "Okay, I'm coming. I'll get Ronnie." Moments like this helped me keep my mind off the threat.

A couple of days after I got home, Chief Langdon called. "Jim, Halpin and I had a powwow with the Crime Scene Investigators."

I interrupted. "Powwow? What are you talking about?"

"Sorry. We met with the CSI team to discuss the details of the evidence."

"What did they find?"

"Several things. There's a good tire exemplar — a fingerprint of a tire track. This could be important. Once the tire print has been analyzed, it can be traced to the exact tire. Now, bear with me. We don't have a suspect and the tire track could be nothing more than a cemetery work vehicle."

"I don't understand, Chief. There are hundreds of brands of tires. How can it be traced back to a particular vehicle?"

"It's a little complicated. No need to get into the details, but here's the basics. A snapshot is taken of the tire prints. From the pictures, we can determine the tire size and weight of the vehicle."

I switched the phone to the other ear. The kids were banging on the piano. "What happens next?"

"As I said, it gets complicated. You don't want—"

"Yes, I do want to know what happens next." I heard Chief inhale, then exhale. I had a feeling he didn't want to continue, but it didn't matter what he wanted.

"If we find a suspect, we'll take a look at what he's driving. The investigator will analyze the tire tracks to see if it matches the prints taken at the cemetery.

I moved to a barstool in the kitchen to get away from the noise of the triplets. I asked Chief to wait until I changed phones. "Okay. Go ahead."

"Lifting a print is like a photo copy of the tire track. Here's how it's done. They lay down a ten to twelve-foot sheet of butcher paper allowing them to get an exact rotation of the tire. Vaseline is used to grease the tread. The vehicle is slowly driven over the paper leaving a gooey trail. Next the tracks are dusted with magnetic powder to lift and preserve the print. An impression specialist will examine the results. He's looking for wear marks on the rubber. We match the tire with a vehicle, that's hard evidence."

"You said you found several clues. What else do you have?"

"CSI found a partial shoeprint, but there was a screw up with the dental stone."

Reaching for the coffee pot, I poured a cup and splashed some on the counter. "Okay, Chief, again, speak in language I can understand."

"Simply put, a cast or dental stone is made of the shoe imprint. Much like your dentist makes a mold of your teeth. The print is absorbed into the cast. Unfortunately, the mold was broken."

"So, why not go back and get another sample of the print."

"Doesn't work that way. Once the print is absorbed into the cast, it's gone from the ground. When the CSI team broke the mold, the imprint was lost. So… nothing to help us."

"Oh, that's just wonderful." I freshened my coffee and knocked it over before I could take a sip. "Any other bad news?"

"No, but we did get lucky. They found the bullet. It was lodged in a tree and in very good condition."

"And?"

"When a round is fired from a gun, the rifling in the barrel leaves grooves on the bullet. No two barrels are alike. So, find the gun that shot the bullet, tie the gun to the owner, now you got something."

"Not much to work with, is it Chief?"

"I disagree. The death threat letter and the tire tracks could be good leads. But, the bullet could be the most important piece of evidence. Cases have been solved with less information than we have."

My emotions bounced from fear to anger to anxiety. How would I cope with this? Something in Chief's tone gave me great concern, made me ache. When he said cases have been solved with less evidence, I didn't believe him. "What do I do now, Chief Langdon?"

"There's not much Jim. Just let us do our job. We'll get to the bottom of this, I promise."

Langdon's tone, the one that concerned me before, gave me no confidence. None at all.

CHAPTER 11

JIM

ONLY MY IMMEDIATE SUPERVISOR AND THE CEO OF PHILLIPS Petroleum knew someone wanted to kill me. They were great bosses, representing a solid company, who offered their support — even if it meant returning to Belleville.

Two weeks after the shooting Chief Langdon called and said he and Halpin wanted me back in New Jersey, just for a day. Langdon booked me on an early-in, late-out flight. Praying they had good news and that this nightmare was going away was a pipedream. My gut told me something different.

Langdon met me at the airport in Newark. The weather was even hotter than when I'd left. The rainy summer made the air heavy, and it sat like a cement block on top my chest. The musty smell of decaying foliage reminded me of the day at the cemetery. I struggled to ignore the stench by breathing through my mouth.

Although the drive from Newark to Belleville was only twenty minutes, it gave me plenty of time to relive the shooting. My shoulders tensed, my breaths grew shorter, and my heart rate became more rapid the closer we got to home. I felt like a soldier returning to battle.

Fear held new meaning for me. It wrapped barbed tentacles around my soul and ripped it from my body. I had to fight every day just to keep my sanity.

Halpin was waiting for us when we arrived at the Belleville police station. I entered the office and he stood to greet me. For some reason I felt safe, secure in his presence, as if his professionalism eased my anxiety.

"Thanks for coming. I'll get right to it." He motioned to a chair and Halpin held up a plastic bag. "This is the bullet we found at the cemetery."

"Definitely not a .22." My back went lightning rod straight and my voice cracked.

Halpin shook his head and handed me the bag. "The round came from a hunting rifle… the type used to hunt deer. I think this is a .30 caliber. Forensics will determine if I'm right. That may take some time depending on their caseload."

I handed the bag back. "What kind of gun would fire that bullet?"

"Right now, my best guess is a Remington M-40 Model 700." Halpin sat on the edge of Langdon's desk.

I had no idea what all this gun talk meant, but Halpin definitely had my attention. "What are you thinking? What does it mean?"

Halpin removed a stick of Big Red from his pocket, unwrapped it, and slid it into his mouth. "American snipers used this rifle in Vietnam. The Marines almost exclusively fired the Model 700." He wadded up the gum wrapper and tossed it into a trash can, then cleared his throat. "I went back out to the cemetery. I happened to look down at one of the granite markers and etched in stone, as if it were a message for me, were the words 'The truth shall seek you out.'" He held up the plastic bag with the bullet, bounced it up and down a few times. "This bullet is the truth… and I'm going to seek out this scumbag."

Chief Langdon poured himself a cup of coffee and walked to the window. "Finding the bullet is a significant part of the puzzle."

The look in Halpin's dark, penetrating eyes made me wonder if he knew something that I didn't know. Something I might not want to know.

Halpin sat in a chair, crossed his legs, then rested his thumb and index finger on his chin. "Do you know what Anderson did after high school?"

I shook my head. "No idea." My intuition told me he knew exactly what Phil Anderson did after we graduated. I wanted no part of this conversation, but at the same time, I needed to know everything.

"After high school, he joined the service and served with the Marines in Vietnam." Halpin's hundred-yard stare went right through me. The detective shifted his head toward Langdon, then back to me. "Phil Anderson was an elite member of the Marine Force Reconnaissance of the 3rd Division. His file indicates he was a good marksman."

My left eye twitched. "Phil bullied me when I first moved to Belleville. I tried to be his friend. Two months later he challenged me after football practice to fight. I took him up on it. Before graduation he attacked me with a baseball bat and swung at my knees after I signed a football scholarship. If you think he's the shooter, all

I ask is give me five minutes alone with him. Let us go bone on bone."

"Hold on." Halpin extended his right hand, palm out. "There's no evidence Anderson did anything. We can pick him up for questioning, and that's what we'll do. Believe me, we'll get to the bottom of this. Just hang tight."

"But, you just said he was a sniper. Who else could it be?"

"No, I said he was a reconnaissance Marine and a good marksman. That's not an indictment of him."

"Well, if he's not a sniper, what's this reconnaissance thing?"

He scratched his head. "Phil was part of a team of six to eight men who infiltrated enemy territory and gathered information. Their goal was to stay off the radar. If a shot had to be fired, it's likely the team wouldn't make it out."

I slapped the chair arms with both hands. They told me things that indicated Phil Anderson was the one. In my mind, they had enough information to go after the jerk. "Okay, okay. I'll let you do your job. Find out if Anderson is the one and put an end to this."

CHAPTER 12

DETECTIVE HALPIN

Forensics left a message with my office that a Dr. Steinhofer had the results on the bullet found at the cemetery in Belleville. I drove across Newark to the lab. The old gray stone building looked like the setting for an Alfred Hitchcock movie. The gothic archways and old wooden window frames were classic nineteenth century architecture in Europe. I expected to see Dr. Frankenstein sitting at a lab table with Bunsen burners and glass beakers.

I descended two flights of dimly-lit concrete stairs to the basement. A mission statement was posted by the door. *All analyses will be performed with the utmost ethics and integrity in the pursuit of truth never forgetting that individual lives are affected by our work.*

I grasped the old, round brass door knob and pulled. Creak, creak, creak. I stepped inside.

Footsteps coming around the corner seemed headed my way. My mind flashed images of a middle-aged man with frizzed silver-white hair and thick round glasses. The steps got closer and closer.

Whoa! The mad German scientist turned out to be a blonde bombshell in her late twenties. Wow. Stunning was an understatement. She had the body of a track athlete. Her smile melted me into a blob of Jell-O.

"Detective Halpin?"

I nodded.

"I'm Dr. Steinhofer. Come on back. I have the bullet for you."

At least I had the German scientist part right. Following her was a treat in itself.

Steinhofer picked up a plastic bag from her desk and turned. "The bullet is a .308 NATO sniper round fired from a rifle with a medium heavy barrel. Probably a Remington Model 700."

"Ah, I was right. Do I need to sign out to take the evidence with me?"

"Nope. I've logged it assigned it to you. We know where it is. You're good to go."

I was in no hurry to leave, but couldn't think of anything to say about the case. The young doctor definitely started my day in the right direction.

Needed to get back to my office and phone Chief Langdon with the update on the bullet.

"Chief Langdon, Detective Halpin here. I was right about the bullet found at the cemetery. It's a .308 NATO sniper round."

I could hear the squeaking of what sounded like a chair. "Great. Now we've got something to work with."

I loosened the knot on my tie and switched the phone to my right hand. "I've also got some interesting background on Anderson. He was released from the Marines with an honorable discharge. The guy's going to Rutgers University and will have enough hours to graduate in… let's see… maybe a year."

"What's his job now?"

"Works nights as a bouncer at a dive bar in Newark. And get this… never been arrested."

"Really?"

I sat down in my chair, crossed my legs and noticed my socks didn't match. One was black, the other brown. How in the heck did that happen? "There's no record of even a traffic violation. This guy's cleaner than a nun at a pick-pocket convention. One other thing, Anderson's coaching a Pee-Wee football team."

"I don't get it. Nothing adds up. He's no choir boy, but with what we have, we can't get a warrant."

I picked up several paper clips scattered on my desk and put them in my drawer. "You're right, Chief. There's not enough evidence to ask a judge for an arrest warrant. Personal issues between the two mean nothing at this point, but I'll visit with the guy and ask him to come to the station to answer a few questions. I'll keep you posted."

After lunch I headed out to Phil Anderson's place. He lived on Willoughby Street. That part of blue-collar Newark was old and run down. His house, like most of the others, looked like a candidate for demolition. The windows were blocked with broken venetian blinds and the front door glass was covered in aluminum foil. In the driveway was a green Jeep with a dented fender and torn rag top that belonged in an auto graveyard where cars went to die.

Should be an interesting meeting. I pushed the cracked, grungy doorbell.

Nothing happened.

Pushed it again.

Silence.

I slid a piece of Big Red into my dry mouth.

After several hard knocks on the paint-chipped door frame, footsteps approached on what sounded like hardwood floors. The warped door jammed as the person on the other side struggled to yank it open. The smell escaping the room had an oily odor, one that I couldn't place.

A muscular man in a sleeveless white T-shirt faced me. His high cheek bones and off-centered nose were framed by short black facial hair. He said nothing, but his cold, viper-like eyes suggested strangers were not welcomed. He wiped his hands on a dingy white towel exposing his hairy knuckles and dirty finger nails.

I removed my sunglasses. "Phillip Anderson?"

The man continued wiping his hands as he moved his head from side to side, sizing me up. "Who wants to know?" His waffle-lipped smile exposed the gap between his two front teeth.

I was trained to deal with guys like this, and even I wouldn't want to meet him in an alley.

I flashed my police badge. "Sean Halpin, Detective with the Newark Police Department."

"What can I do for you?" The tone of his voice was much friendlier.

"Do you know a Jim Pepperman?"

Phil nodded. "Went to high school with a Jim Pepperman. What's this about?"

"Someone took a shot at him. We're contacting people that knew Jim, trying to get leads on who did it."

Phil angled his head and squinted. "Am I a suspect?"

I took the gum from my mouth, placed it in an empty wrapper, slipped it into my pocket and smiled. "No, no, no. Just trying to get information, that's all."

Phil slapped his towel over one shoulder and leaned against the door frame. "Do you have a warrant?" His slowly pronounced words turned sour again.

My mouth was tight, the corners turned up. I'd been around this sucker for five minutes and knew I didn't like him. "No, sir. Just want to ask you a few questions."

I'd learned to read people and trusted my instincts. The casual body slouch, arrogant manner, and the facial smirks were all negative vibes. I knew not to trust this guy.

"Well, then I don't have to answer your questions, do I?" Anderson's voice was a little too cocky for my liking.

I felt my nerves tingle up and down my body. This guy knew how to play hardball. He was doing everything he could to push my buttons, and it was working. I had to slow my emotions and remain calm. I shook my head, forcing a smile. "No, you don't."

Anderson crossed his arms and straightened. "What will happen if I don't answer your questions?"

He provided me with an opening to hit back. I gave him a hard look, a look I knew he would understand. "I'll get that warrant."

Phil laughed. It wasn't a funny laugh, but a wicked one, high pitched, and loud. "I guess I have no choice, do I?"

"Nope," I unwrapped a fresh piece of gum.

"Come on in Detective. I'm just giving you a hard time. I'll be glad to answer your questions." His mood was suddenly relaxed, like he enjoyed our bantering.

Entering the house, I noticed several deer heads mounted on the walls and a gun rack with three rifles. I watched Phil's back as he went to the kitchen. His heavy, thick legs suggested he was an athlete. I heard water running.

"Looks like you're a hunter," I said over the water.

He snorted a condescending grunt. "What makes you say that, Officer?"

This guy was in full game mode. I was a detective, not an officer, and he knew that.

I gave him a dose of payback sarcasm. "I guess it's the dead animal parts on your wall and the three rifles next to them." The wise-off.

Phil returned, drying his hands. He drug his feet across the hardwood floor. "You a hunter, Officer?"

"No, tried it once. Had a buck in my sight, but couldn't pull the trigger."

Phil tucked his chin and smiled. "Buck fever... happens to some hunters."

I pointed to the weapons. "What kind of rifles are those?"

"The top one is a .243 Winchester bolt action. The next is a lever action .3030. The bottom one, my favorite, is a Remington Model 700."

I had to deadpan my emotions. The Remington with a modified barrel could fire a NATO grain bullet like the one from the cemetery. "Why is that your favorite?"

The smile left Anderson's bristly face as he walked to the gun rack and removed the Remington. He turned toward me, holding the rifle across his chest with a look that would scare Big Foot. Phil's eyes were wide open, but he wasn't seeing me. Anderson appeared to be reliving something. "I had some buddies in Vietnam who were snipers, and they killed hundreds of those little gook bastards with a rifle like this one."

I didn't have to hear the hate in his voice. I could see it in his face. It was as though his mind went back to a dark secret hell.

A lump forced its way into my throat, and perspiration dotted my upper lip. The room suddenly felt damp, like a mausoleum filled with coffins.

To deflect his mood, I walked toward Anderson and asked to look at the rifle. I could see it didn't have the medium-heavy barrel needed to handle the .308 NATO round that was fired at Pepperman. "This is a nice rifle. I can tell you're proud of it… no finger smudges on the stock or barrel."

Phil took the rifle from me and put it back in the rack. "I take care of all my guns. Now, what are your questions?"

I had to get Anderson on my territory. The police station gave me the best opportunity to get the information I needed. "Let's go to the station and talk. Is that okay with you?"

"I'm not wild about police stations, but I've got nothing to hide. I'll come in and answer your questions. Let's get this over."

"Oh, that oily smell. I can't put my finger on it. What is it, Mr. Anderson?"

"Linseed oil. I'm putting a new stock on one of my rifles. I hand rub it on the unfinished wood to give it that shiny look."

"What rifle are you talking about? One of the three in the gun rack… or another one?"

CHAPTER 13

DETECTIVE HALPIN

I'D INTERVIEWED DOZENS OF PEOPLE AND HAD A HUNCH Anderson was going to be tough. He had street smarts. Those types often anticipated the questions and had quick, believable responses, but I looked forward to the challenge.

Mr. Anderson was placed in The Box, a room used for questioning at the Newark Police Station. The cubical was small, 12 x 12, with an anchored table and one chair. I asked, "Can I get you a cup of coffee, water, or a soda?"

He pulled the chair away from the table and took a seat facing me. "Sure, I'll take a pink lemonade with lots of ice."

Right on cue—cocky and self-assured. I wasn't going to let him tick me off and control the interview. I gave him a smile, not a disrespectful in-your-face smile, not even an I'm-better-than-you smile, just a calming, in-control smile. "Sorry, how about a soda?"

He gave me an index finger salute. He knew I got the best of him. "A soda would be good."

I left the room to get the drink and observed his body language through the one-way mirror along with two other detectives. He showed no signs of stress. His legs were still, no bouncing up and down, feet flat on the floor, no nervous reactions with his arms. This guy was as cool as a refrigerated beer truck.

Returning to the interrogation room, I handed Phil his soft drink. He took it with his right hand. Right-handed people were more apt to be linear thinkers. They thought and acted in specific patterns.

I placed a clipboard on the edge of the desk and asked him to sign the information form. He did so, then slid the papers back to the corner.

When people wanted to conceal something, they often put an object in front of them to act as a buffer between themselves and the person doing the questioning. Returning the clipboard to the corner of the table could indicate he had nothing to hide.

I folded my hands behind me and rested against the dull green door frame. "Tell me about your relationship with Jim Pepperman."

Phil's elbows were resting on the arms of the chair, feet still anchored on the floor. "What do you want to know?"

"Did the two of you get along?"

"No."

"Why not?"

"First time I saw him, there was something I didn't like. He was the new guy in town, wore those dumb cowboy boots, spoke with a Texas twang. I thought he got me kicked off the football team. No chance for me to get a scholarship when that happened."

"Do you still feel like he got you kicked off the team?"

Phil shook his head. "No."

"Why?"

"Detective, that was a long time ago. My life was in shambles. My parents fought all the time and eventually got a divorce. I blamed everyone for my problems. Jim didn't get me kicked off the team. My attitude did. I wouldn't admit it then, but I was responsible for most of my bad behavior, and that's the truth."

The room was hot, no windows, with little ventilation. I rolled up my sleeves. "Where were you last Sunday from three 'til six?"

"At the pistol range in Belleville."

"Wow... that's a long time firing a weapon."

Phil tapped his fingers on the table and grinned. "I only shot for thirty minutes or so. A bunch of us old vets go across the street and tell war stories at Tiny's Bar."

"Can you prove you were at the shooting range and the bar?"

Phil leaned forward, rested his forearms on the table and looked me in the eye. "Yes. The manager, Vince Worth, talked with me when I signed in."

I rubbed the back of my stiff neck. Falling asleep in the recliner watching TV last night was stupid. "You served in Vietnam, didn't you?"

"Yes, sir, the 3rd Marines."

"What was your job?"

"Reconnaissance."

I tilted my head and lowered my chin. "What does that mean?" I knew the answer, but wanted him to talk, maybe catch him in a lie.

"I was inserted behind enemy lines with five other guys to do surveillance."

"Surveillance? Tell me about it."

"Our mission was to gather intelligence."

"So you were never directly involved in fire fights... actually killing the enemy."

"Our mission was to never be detected. If we were discovered and captured, it meant certain death. Recon teams have been captured.... You don't want to know what happened to them."

What were Phil's true emotions about his military service in Vietnam? At his house, I got the impression he liked killing.

"Can you be more specific about gathering intelligence?"

Phil's body language changed. His arms were drawn close to his sides, hands cupped in front of him, eyes dead as the proverbial door knob. It was as though he had a hollow feeling buried in the pit of his stomach that wouldn't go away. His body was in Newark, his mind — some place horrible.

"When they dropped us behind enemy lines, we were totally alone. Silence was an absolute. We communicated by sign language or whispering. Most missions lasted two or three days. Our responsibility was to monitor troop movement. Charlie, the enemy, gathered when they planned a coordinated attack. If we could find them all bunched up, we'd call in an airstrike and wipe them out before they had a chance to launch an attack. At the time I got a great deal of pleasure seeing those stinkin' dinks snuffed. To me, they were nothing more than vermin, not worth a second thought. Detective, what do you know about napalm?"

"Ah… not much. Weren't they fire bombs?"

Phil gritted his teeth, relaxed, then took a gulp of his drink. "It's an anti-personnel weapon. Napalm is a mixture of a gelling substance and petroleum… smells like gasoline. Every time I fill up my Jeep, it reminds me of napalm." Sweat beaded on his forehead.

This guy was reliving a dark time.

He took another big swallow. "When it comes into contact with skin… the skin melts off the bones. It's like roasting your body over an open spit. Do you know what burned human flesh smells like after a few days?"

I shook my head.

"Like barbeque." He paused and stared at me. His eyes were lifeless. No emotion. "The lucky ones died instantly… others suffered unmercifully. I witnessed this and, at the time, took pleasure knowing the Viet Cong and the North Vietnamese Army were exposed to this man-made hell."

I knew what he was going through. I'd had friends experience the same kind of trauma.

"After I returned from Nam, the nightmares began. I smelled burning flesh. Heard the screams. I used drugs and alcohol as a crutch to forget the past. Didn't work. The enemy I once hated, I saw as ordinary people with parents, wives, brothers, and sisters. I couldn't get past the thought… why were good men on each side doing this to one another?"

God, I hate what war does to people.

Phil leaned back and covered his face with his hands. It seemed as though he was trying to conceal the shame buried deep in his soul. Then, his hands slowly retreated to his mouth and stopped. " At one point, I held a gun to my head." His words were muffled by his fingers. "I couldn't stand one more sleepless night seeing people sacrificed for nothing."

"What did you do to exorcise the demons?"

"I was lucky to have a friend that led me to a priest. He gave me counseling and guided me to the VA hospital in D.C. which also helped. Most of the time I can control my demons, but sometimes they surface, and I get pleasure thinking about Vietnam. When you were in my house looking at the rifles, for a split second, I relived that excitement. Thankfully, God pulls me out of that dark hole and refuses to let me dwell in that twisted state."

Mesmerized with Anderson's story, my gut said he was telling the truth. However, one thing bugged me. All the rifles on the gun rack had well-kept, wooden stocks. Why was he making a new stock and for what rifle?

"Thanks for your coming in. I have no other questions at this time."

Phil pushed himself away from the table. "Okay, hope I've helped you out. Check you later, Detective."

Anderson had told me a compelling, believable story about his life. He was either telling the truth or he was a pathological liar. Was he capable of killing another human being? I didn't know — I just didn't know.

CHAPTER 14

DETECTIVE HALPIN

THE NEXT MORNING I CALLED LANGDON FROM MY OFFICE before 8 a.m. hoping he was at work. I had to talk above the office chatter about the Yankees. "Chief Langdon, Halpin here. I wanted to keep you updated on my questioning of Phil Anderson yesterday. He cooperated fully."

I eased my reading glasses on and took a bite of a Bavarian cream donut. "Chief, my donut just exploded all over my desk calendar. Give me a minute." I smothered the sticky filling with my handkerchief, then plopped it into the waste basket. Also trashed the current month calendar and the pencil covered with the filling. I hoped no one saw my mishap. The cat calls and laughter answered that question. I gave them the "up yours" sign.

"Do I think he was honest?" It sounded like Langdon was skeptical.

"After the interview, my first impressions would have to be yes. I observed him alone, no nervous twitching with his legs or arms. His voice level never changed. No pitch increase at all during the interview. I watched his eye movement associated with right-handed people. It was consistent with telling the truth."

"Did he have an alibi?"

"Yes…. He was at a gun range Sunday afternoon in Belleville. I talked with the manager, and he said he was there. He even showed me where Anderson signed in and out. At this point, he's clean."

I removed my reading glasses and closed Anderson's file. I picked up my ballpoint and twirled it between my fingers, considering the next move. "Let's get Jim on a conference call."

CHAPTER 15

JIM

My day was shot after the call with Halpin and Langdon. At least, I didn't have to fly back to New Jersey. After putting the boys to bed, Laura descended the stairs and paused on the landing. Her blank, lifeless stare and drooped shoulders could be fatigue, but I suspected it was emotional stress.

I motioned for her to sit with me on the sofa in the living room. Our eyes locked. I had to give her some reassurance we would get through this crisis. But how? How could I protect my family and keep a semblance of order and sanity in the midst of uncertainty and chaos?

Picking up Laura's hand, I turned toward her. "Our lives have changed. We have two choices. One is to stand strong in our faith, or we can play the role of victims and hunker down in fear. We're not in control of our lives, God is. Are we going to trust Him?"

Laura jerked her hand from mine and pulled both knees up to her chest. Her eyes seemed to shrink. "Are you telling me we're to do nothing, just sit back and let all this play out? What if this sicko succeeds in killing you? Am I to throw up my hands and think, oh, well, this is

God's plan? The boys and I will just have to adjust our lives without you." She fingered with the locket I had given her on our first anniversary. "Is that what you're saying?" She'd lost weight. Her pale skin emphasized the circles under her eyes. Signs of defeat.

I moved closer, caressing her face in my hands. "No, I'm going to fight and so are you. We've got to take every precaution. Be aware of what's going on around us. Take no chances. The house will be secured with an alarm system this week.

"And," I dreaded saying the words, "I'm getting a gun."

She doubled her fist and pounded my chest, harder and harder. "You know how I feel about guns. Not in this house."

I slammed my open hand on the sofa cushion and walked to the window, looked out, then turned. "What would you have me do? I can't protect myself against someone who has a weapon.... I have no choice."

The room was quiet, so quiet I could hear the wall clock in the hallway.

She wiped a tear from her cheek with the back of her hand. "Look what this is doing to us, Jim. We're at each other's throat. How are we going to get through this? How on earth are we going to get through this?"

I returned to the couch. My heart going ka-boom, ka-boom. Couldn't let Laura know my true feelings. "I won't kowtow, and you won't either. We'll fight and do whatever we have to do until the guy is caught. Look, my butt's on the goal line with fourth and one. The guy succeeds, game's over. It's not gonna happen.... No way."

"Lord, help us." Her voice inched up an octave and her words light. "Your life's been threatened, and you think of it like a challenge from your football days." Her words changed the direction of our conversation and put a little air in our deflated lives.

I stifled a chuckle. The moment still tense. "That's the way I'm wired. Someone comes at me, I'll take him out." I pulled Laura's head next to my chest. "You are the anchor and strength of this family. Without you, I'm nothing. We'll survive this threat — we will survive."

I'd been unaware of house noises before now. The creaking, cracking, and moaning of the wooden studs were haunting. Each two-by-four communicated with the others in a chilling way.

Getting up and checking on the boys had become a nightly routine. Along with checking the doors and windows. Every waking moment consumed my thoughts about someone wanting to kill me. How would it end? Exhausted, mentally drained — I would eventually doze off.

My middle of the night dreams flip-flopped between the death threats and the man in the Minnesota alley. I could still see his large, crooked teeth framed by thick, rubbery lips. Why did he follow me out of the bar? I was trying to get away from him.

The next morning I went to the kitchen and poured a cup of coffee. I could hear the boys bustling around upstairs and Laura, I was sure, doing her best to corral the three cubs in an attempt to get them dressed. In the past I took for granted the morning preparation with my kids.

These routine things in life had become special. Hearing their voices filled with joy made me feel blessed. The whining and fussing that used to annoy me were now cherished moments. Why did it take something like this to put everything into perspective? I was ashamed my life had been so self-centered that I'd failed to recognize God's gifts.

The muffled sounds of little feet chugged through the living room toward the kitchen. Chuck reached me first. His round, chubby face had a puzzled look. He folded all five fingers together and tapped his upper lip. "Daddy eat chocolate?"

I smiled and looked at Laura. She ruffled his already messy hair. "No, Chuck, Daddy has a sore. It's not chocolate."

Ronnie tugged on Laura's pajamas. "Mommy, I want sore like Daddy."

While scratching his backside, Leon added, "Me too… want sore like Daddy."

"I declare Jim, you're fever blister seems to be the hit of the day," Laura said in a low, whispering voice.

I grinned and took a sip of my Saturday morning coffee. At that moment life seemed normal, and for a brief instant, the thought of a death threat vanished.

Noticing the postal truck siding up to the mail box, I laid down the newspaper and walked outside. The stiffness in my knees was not unusual for this time of day. Football injuries were a reminder of my age.

The junk advertisements were a constant, but one piece of mail stood out. *Jim Pepperman* was spelled out in blue stick-on letters and the postmark—New York

City. My hands shook. I tried to swallow, but couldn't. Looking toward the house and hoping Laura wasn't watching, I jaggedly ripped open the envelope with my forefinger, then unfolded the letter, one crease at a time. The cold, plastic message read:

Pepperman, luck was on your side.

Time's run out.

You've no place to hide.

CHAPTER 16

JIM

I shut the mailbox door and read the death threat again, my eyes darting back and forth across the page. I'd keep this from Laura. I gripped the paper tighter and tapped it on my other hand. No, that wouldn't be right. She needed to know, but how would I tell her?

Glancing up at the house, I saw Laura facing me through the picture window. It was as though she could read the note. Her slumped shoulders and expressionless face were a dead giveaway.

I labored toward the front porch.

She opened the door and stepped outside, meeting me on the steps "What's wrong?"

I handed her the letter and watched her trembling fingers, eyes fixated on the folded piece of paper. Laura opened one section, then the other, her face pale and her lips parted. "My God, what are we going to do?"

I took the letter and gently embraced her. "I'll call Chief Langdon."

My mind was a floating shipwreck on a sea of disaster. Trying to keep my sanity and being strong for the family was driving me into a dark, swirling undertow. Something had to give, or I was going to snap.

After I called Langdon, I turned to my wife. "Why don't you take the kids and go to Philadelphia and visit Penny? Get away from all this for a while."

Laura placed her hands on my face. "No, I'm not leaving you, and besides, I don't want to impose on Penny."

"Honey, just call. Penny's your friend. You two were roommates in nursing school, and she'll be glad to see you, especially if she knows the circumstances." I gently removed her hands from my face and kissed her on the forehead.

The stress on Laura had taken its toll. Her skin was ashen, her eyes hollow. Warmth and happiness had all but disappeared from her face.

Anger ripped at my stomach for what this was doing to Laura and paranoia latched on to me. That SOB would pay—one way or another.

CHAPTER 17

LAURA

Penny told me to pack up the boys and head to Philadelphia. Thank goodness for close relationships. She didn't even ask why I needed to come. A few days away from this caldron of pressure might ease some of my anxiety. I hated being vulnerable. And the emotional tension was wearing on me.

Penny picked us up at the airport. Back at her apartment, the kids were settled in for a nap, and our conversation turned to the real reason for the visit. We went outside on her patio with a glass of Pinot Noir.

"I've got something to tell you." My hands twitched out of control. "It sounds bizarre to say it out loud, but someone tried to kill Jim."

Penny sat motionless, eyes wide with shock. "Someone tried to kill Jim? Are you serious?" She placed a hand over her mouth, then dropped it. "Of course you're serious. Go on."

"Jim was at his dad's gravesite in Belleville when someone shot at him."

Penny moved her patio chair next to mine. "Do they have any idea who it was? And who would want to kill Jim?"

I dug a tissue from my pocket and dabbed the corners of my eyes. I wanted Penny to know what was happening, but it was gut-wrenching to tell the story. "That's what the police are trying to find out. There've been two death threat notes. I'm jumpy, restless, and scared."

Penny cradled both my hands. "Jim and the police will figure this out.... They will. I'm so glad you thought of me. Happy to have you and the boys here as long as you want. What can I do to help you?"

"You're already doing it. Jim wanted me to step away from the madness for a while. Right now, I need a friend to lean on."

"You've got it, hon. I'm here for you as long as it takes. You're worn out, especially after travelling with three little motion machines. Would you like another glass of wine?"

"Yes... please." I finished off the first glass.

"Come with me to the kitchen. It's a cozy place to talk. I put some brie en croute in the oven."

I paused, not sure what brie en croute was. "Explain that in English, please."

"That's the fancy name for brie cheese wrapped in puff pastry dough."

I folded and unfolded a flowered napkin at the kitchen table. My nervous energy was constant. "It's been so long since we had a visit. I've lost track of what's happening in your life. Do you still have the same job?"

"Well... ," Penny turned toward me with a smile that needed no explanation. "I got a promotion. Head surgical nurse at Temple University Hospital. Wanted that position for years. But, now that I have it… not sure I have the right stuff."

"Come on, you're a great nurse. What's got you ruffled?"

"Jeez, don't know where to start. I don't get much respect from the hospital administrator, but the added responsibility is the toughest."

"You were the best surgical nurse in Philadelphia when I was here. You'll be fine. In a year or two you'll wonder why you ever doubted yourself."

Setting the puff pastries on the table, Penny poured a second glass of wine. She cocked her head like she was bursting with a secret.

"What?" I asked.

"I'm also seeing a new guy, a cardio-vascular surgeon. He moved here from Baltimore. We've been going out nearly six months, and every date's been fantastic. He's very handsome. Looks just like that actor who played Dr. Kildare on TV. Who was that guy?"

I returned Penny's smile and tapped my head. "Richard Chamberlain."

Penny nodded. "I could hardly wait for the scenes he was in. What a great face. I even had a Dr. Kildare shirt. Did you have one?"

"Yes. Thought I was something special wearing that white, button up the side shirt, with that little standup collar. What was I thinking? Oh, Penny, tell me about your new guy."

"Well." She took a sip of her wine. "He was raised on a farm in central Nebraska. His father's a country veterinarian." She lifted her glass, little finger extended. "You know what else?"

I laughed lightly, sure she'd tell me even if I didn't ask. "No, but I think you're going to tell me."

"His father delivered him, right there in the family house. His dad told him it was a lot easier delivering a colt. Isn't that a unique thing in this day and age? Born in your own house and delivered by your dad."

"Does he have a name?"

"He does." Penny snickered. "And a good one, too. Brad... Bradley Jameson." She clasped her hands over her heart. "He's the best man I've ever met, and you know how picky I am. Waiting for Mr. Right... and this could be him."

"How exciting." I softened my voice. "Do you ever see Neal Sullivan at the hospital?"

Penny hesitated. "Used to, but not anymore. He moved."

"Did he ever marry?" I quizzed.

"Not while he was here. You breaking the engagement just before the wedding really did a number on him."

"Surely he realized we weren't meant for each other. Even if we had married, it wouldn't have lasted."

"Why? What makes you think so?"

"Finally realized I was in love with his status as a doctor, not him. With Jim, it was different. I loved him, not his football career."

"Why did you bring up Neal? That all happened a long time ago. What was it, seven years or so?"

"Yes. You know how it kills me to hurt someone, and I realize the timing was rotten. Carried that guilt ever since. I hoped that he would have found someone who could love him for who he is."

"Quit blaming yourself. You did what you had to do."

"About six weeks before the wedding, I found myself thinking about Jim all the time. That didn't seem right. Then one day I admitted to myself, Jim was the man I loved. The man I wanted to be with." I leaned across the table. "You'll never believe what I did," I whispered.

Penny cocked her head. "What did you do, Laura?"

"Jim had moved to Bartlesville, Oklahoma, and I was in Philadelphia. I called him and said I would break my engagement if he would marry me."

"Get out of here."

"I really did. Cross my heart." I sat back in the chair and lowered my eyes. "I had to tell Neal I was going to marry Jim. I felt so sorry for him, but what else could I do?"

Penny tapped her fingernails on her glass. "Because you're my friend, I need to tell you… he carried a lot of resentment about the break-up."

"Neal told you that?"

"No, he didn't tell me. It was water cooler conversation. According to the gossip, he blamed you for ruining his life. If the rumors were true, his anger sounded dangerous. But hey, you know how talk can be exaggerated. Probably nothing to it, nothing at all." Penny's voice should have been light and dismissive.

Instead, it was serious. Dead serious.

CHAPTER 18

LAURA

I MOVED BACK TO THE LIVING ROOM COUCH, KICKED OFF MY shoes, and pulled my legs up under me. "Oh, I almost forgot. The boys need diapers. Is there a grocery store nearby?"

Water sloshed in the sink. "Sure," Penny answered from the kitchen. "Only a few blocks from here. Let me finish the dishes, and I'll go get some."

I adjusted the couch cushion. "I need a stretch. A short walk would do me good. If you don't mind while the boys are sleeping."

Penny entered the living room, drying her hands. "Okay, be glad to watch the triplets. When you exit the apartment building, turn left. The store's three blocks down the street, and there's a great coffee shop inside."

I nodded. "Thanks, Penny. Thanks for being a good friend." The day had been long, and I was relieved to have a few minutes to myself.

Penny's neighborhood was dotted with upscale apartments and a park across the street. A group of kids played baseball. They couldn't have been more than nine or ten. One boy reminded me of Jim—tall, muscular and short blond hair. The spitting image of Jim at that age, I was sure.

The sun slipped behind the trees edging the sidewalk. It would be dark soon. The evening air closed in and a sudden chill caused me to shiver.

I needed this trip to Philadelphia. The walk allowed me to step away from all the negativity. The death threats had taken their toll, and I was unraveling on the inside. Before the shooting, Jim had nightmares. Something had been wrong, even then. Something he wouldn't tell me.

The store was new and well lit. The coffee shop Penny talked about had the ambiance of a Paris restaurant with straight-back wooden chairs, white cotton table cloths, and the classic French love song "La Vie en Rose" playing in the background. The waiters were dressed in white shirts, black pants and bow ties, with long red aprons snuggly tight around their waists.

"Could I help you?" the server asked in a French accent.

I smiled on the inside. Nice touch for a Philadelphia business. I ordered a cream soda made fresh at the open area beverage bar. The cool drink tasted of fresh cream mixed with the right amount of carbonation and soda.

After taking a sip of the soft drink, I noticed a man across the store who reminded me of Neal. Penny said he'd moved from Philadelphia to Chicago a few years ago. Neal didn't cross my mind often, but I still felt guilty about the break-up. He was a good person and deserved to be with someone who cared about him the way I never could. I hoped Penny was wrong about his bitterness toward me. That was seven years ago. Surely he'd gotten over it.

I looked at my watch. I'd been there an hour. When I left home, Jim reminded me not be out after dark.

I picked up the diapers and stepped outside. A strange feeling locked onto me. There was no traffic. The moon was full, and a thin line of clouds drifted over the bright surface. A sudden burst of wind stirred up dust and a small piece of paper tumbled end over end coming to rest against the curb.

I looked across the street. Not one person. I clutched the diapers under my arm and walked toward Penny's apartment. Still, no one on the street. What was going on? My heart rate increased.

The street lights were hazy, like a fog had moved in and smothered the city. A small dog sprinted across the street and down a dark, narrow alley. What was he running from? The feeling of being alone frightened me.

I paused, turned, and looked behind me. A man stood under the dim street light. He was too far away for me to describe him, but I felt he was staring at me. What do I do?

If I ran it might embolden him. Instead, I worked hard to walk at a normal pace, my pulse double-timing, my breathing exaggerated. Be calm. Be calm. I had to be calm.

After taking a few steps, I looked back. He was gone. I exhaled a welcomed sigh of relief. My fear had been for nothing. I was ashamed for reacting like a silly teenager.

I smiled thinking about the mystery man and telling the story to Penny. It would be a funny ending to a long day.

CHAPTER 19

LAURA

I FUMBLED THROUGH MY PURSE LOOKING FOR THE CODE TO enter Penny's building. Where had I put it? Ah, there it was behind my billfold.

I looked up. The reflection on the glass door exposed a man standing behind me. Cold, shark-like eyes showed no emotion. Neal. Neal was here. I hadn't been imagining him.

I spun around. "Oh my gosh, Neal you scared me." I placed my hand over my heart and tried to calm down.

"Laura, I thought it was you at the coffee shop." His tone was low and throaty. Not friendly like he was glad to see me.

One look at his face, the dejected eyes, flared nostrils, told me I was in trouble.

He touched my hair, rubbing it between his fingers. "Why did you cut it?" Then he placed his hands of either side of my head, trapping me to the door. He leaned in close and his breath reeked of hard liquor. "You know how I loved those long curls."

My body shook. I straightened against the door to deaden the trembling. I swallowed trying to gain composure. I had to get him thinking about something other than me. "Heard you moved to Chicago."

He nodded. "I did, but I come back once a month... consulting with a surgical clinic. My condo is a few blocks from the grocery store."

He looked down, then up at me, fondling me with his stare. It was disgusting.

Fear oozed from every pore of my rigid body.

His mouth was tight, jaw locked. Then he relaxed. "How's the family?"

He asked a question, but I knew he couldn't care less. He was playing word games. Didn't like him bringing my family into the discussion.

My heart pounded so hard I could hear it. Something needed to change the direction of our conversation. "Neal, sounds like your career is booming." I struggled to conceal the quiver in my voice.

His chin dipped, eyes turned upward. "It's going very well. I spend the majority of my time working.... Not much time for a social life. But, hey, who needs a companion when you're earning the kind of money I do?"

The barb was directed at me. A reminder of the broken engagement.

He paused, made a clicking sound with his tongue. "Well... I've got things to do." When he reached the curb, he turned to face me, and tapped a cigarette on its case. After lighting it, Neal took a long, slow drag and exhaled. With a thin straight line grin he said, "Good to see you, Laura."

The air was like soup, thick and heavy. I watched him cross the street and disappear into the darkness. I cupped my hand over my mouth and wept.

I reached for the keypad, shaking so hard my fingers wouldn't work. What's the number? 2522. No, 2225. Where's the paper with the code? I turned toward the street. No one there. Relax. I punched the number 2225. Didn't work. Tried 2522. The lock clicked open.

I pushed through the door and ran to the elevator. Pressed the up button. Nothing happened. I repeated it. Still nothing. "Come on, you stupid elevator. Come on." The third press, I heard it coming down.

Before stepping in I looked to make sure no one was there. Paranoia had control of me. The slow moving lift took forever to reach the fifth floor. I banged on Penny's door. Hurry, Penny, hurry.

One look at Penny's face, her horrified eyes, told me she knew I was in danger. She pulled me inside the apartment. "What's wrong, Laura?"

I walked to the couch, hands covering my face, and sat rocking, gathering my thoughts. "You won't believe what happened."

She sat next to me on the sofa. "Laura, what?"

"I saw Neal."

"Neal Sullivan?"

"Yes, he followed me from the grocery store. That's not the man I was engaged to marry." I ran my hand through my hair, eyes closed.

"What did he do to you?"

"He pinned me to the door... got in my face. His eyes were dark and small. His rotten breath smelled of cigarettes and bourbon. Oh, the worst part. He stroked my hair. I've never been so repulsed. He tried to make me feel cheap and vulnerable."

"What did he say?"

"Small talk. He pointed to the diapers and asked about my family. It wasn't what he said, but how he said it."

I made a fist and placed it over my mouth. "He tried to intimidate me, but I didn't give him the satisfaction."

"Do you want me to call the police?"

"And tell them what? He didn't do anything. No threats, nothing." I hesitated, biting the corner of my lower lip. "I'll tell you one thing. Neal Sullivan turned out to be a sick individual."

CHAPTER 20

LAURA

Penny sat at the opposite end of the sofa from me. "Laura, I didn't know him well, but that doesn't sound like Neal."

I pulled my knees to my chest and edged into the corner of the couch. "Agree. Totally different. He smokes. That never happened when we were together. Neal hated tobacco. And alcohol. He'd have a glass of wine with a meal and that was it."

Penny moved next to me. "Had he been drinking?"

"His words slurred and the smell of hard liquor was undeniable."

"Maybe that's it. Could have had one too many and it changed his personality. If you were to see him tomorrow, you might feel differently."

"Perhaps, but his eyes.… I'll never forget the look he gave me. That hollow, empty stare. I sensed evil, Penny."

A loud clap of thunder shook the room and the lights flickered. Small patters of rain hit the sliding glass doors to the patio.

Penny pushed from the sofa like a coiled box spring. "Check the windows in your room. I'll close the umbrella on the patio."

One of the windows had been open. I looked at the boys. Sound asleep. I walked back in the living room.

Penny smiled at me. We both laughed, not a funny laugh, but a tension-relief laugh.

I lightly clapped my hands, enjoying the moment. "If we'd been writing a mystery novel, the timing couldn't have been better. Can you believe the thunder crashed when I said Neal was evil?"

"Sherlock Holmes stuff."

Another clap of thunder and lightning skipped across the horizon.

"This storm came in fast." I crossed my arms, rubbing up and down with both hands. "Is that normal?"

"No, but it happens."

A blast of thunder, the lights flickered again—then darkness.

"Stay where you are. I'll get a flashlight." Her steps were brisk, almost robotic.

A bolt of lightning.

The room was cold and eerie. Goose bumps spread over my skin and body.

Light sprang from the kitchen. "I've got a kerosene lantern too. That will give us more light."

"I'm surprised the thunder didn't wake the boys." My eyes pinballed around the living room. "Do you know where I put the diapers?"

"No, but take the flashlight and look in the bedroom. I'll use the lantern to search the living room."

"I've looked here and the bathroom. No luck. How about you?" I called from the bedroom hallway.

"Same here. Nothing."

I remembered. "They're outside. Neal had me so shaken I left them on the steps."

A loud knock shook the door to the apartment.

"It's probably Mrs. Hudson across the hall," Penny said. "She may need to borrow a flashlight."

I heard Penny unlatch the door and release the lock. A cracking of thunder. Then silence. "Laura, come here, now."

"What is it?"

She lowered the lantern toward the box of diapers. The diapers I'd left outside of the building.

CHAPTER 21

LAURA

Penny grabbed the diapers, locked the door, and motioned for me to sit at the kitchen table. Something in her eyes frightened me. It was as if she had no answer for the fear consuming us.

The rain pelted harder against the patio door. The lightning flashes illuminated Penny's face. The flames licked the globe of the kerosene lantern sending broken bits of light across the room.

Cold panic wrapped around my spine. "How did the diapers get there?" I knew the answer, but wished I didn't.

Penny looked at me in silence for what seemed a full minute. She put up her best defensive smile. "I'm sure there's a logical explanation." She avoided eye contact, and I knew she was lying.

"Stop it. You're not helping. Neal put them there. He's stalking me."

"Okay… okay. If Neal wanted to hurt you, he had his chance. But nothing happened. Right?"

I nodded and placed both hands over my eyes and drug my fingers to my chin. "Maybe you're right, but you weren't there when he approached me. I saw the ugliness in him... the fake grin, the drunken flush of his cheeks, and those eyes. They were dead, Penny, cold and hard."

"I'd feel the same as you, but we don't know Neal's intentions."

"I'm scared out of my mind, and you're making excuses for him." I fired a look of disappointment at Penny.

"I'm not, but I'm trying to help you get through this."

I shook my head. "I'm sorry. I know you're trying to help. It's Jim's situation, now this. I'm fried, Penny, and don't know what to do."

"I'm here. You can count on it."

"I know. Thanks for standing by me."

The silence of dead air was shattered by the high-pitched ring of the telephone. Startled, neither of us said a word. The events of the night pulled us back into the unknown. Was it Jim? Was there an emergency at the hospital? Or — was it Neal?

Penny slowly walked to the phone. Her shaking hand reached for the receiver. "Hello... hello. Who is this?" She turned to me.

The bottom dropped out of my stomach and I began to hyperventilate. "Who was it, Penny?"

She shook her head, "I don't know. They hung up."

One of the boys cried out. I went to them, picked Leon up and returned to the living room.

There was a loud knock on the front door. Then another. For a split second time froze. And so did I.

Penny pointed to Leon. "Take him back. I'm getting my gun."

CHAPTER 22

LAURA

Penny rushed to her bedroom and returned with a small silver handgun. I angled my head around the hallway door frame, just enough to see.

A louder knock at the front door.

Any icy blade sliced through my chest.

Penny held the gun by her side. "Who is it? What do you want?"

Silence. Then the lightning and a blast of thunder that rattled the windows.

"Is there anyone there? I'm calling the police if you don't answer."

"Honey, it's Mrs. Hudson."

Penny's head tilted back, shoulders and arms relaxed. "Mrs. Hudson." She turned and looked at me as she slid the gun into her pocket and opened the door. "Please, come in."

The slightly-hunched silver-haired lady snailed her way across the carpet into the living room. "Do you have any flashlight batteries?"

"Let me check." Penny walked to the cabinet in the kitchen, shuffled through a drawer, then turned." Yes, I have a four-pack of D's. Will that work?"

"Oh, that's perfect. You're such a dear."

Penny raked her blonde hair away from her face. "Quite a storm, isn't it, Mrs. Hudson?"

"Yes, I love stormy weather. I could sit and watch the lightning all night. It's calming to me, but the thunder scares Fluffy, my little poodle. I'd better get back." When she reached the door, she turned to Penny. "You're a good friend. Thanks so much."

Penny eased the door shut and locked it, then turned toward me. "Oh, my gosh," she whispered and patted her chest.

There was something about the unknown that could break your spirit. My spirit was melting away like mist in the sunlight.

After thirty minutes the power was restored. Having light made me feel safer. The storm was letting up and that also helped my splintered nerves.

I needed to call Jim. I hoped he would answer the phone. After one ring, I heard his strong voice. "Hello."

"It's Laura." I knew my voice was trembling, but couldn't make it stop. There was a pause.

"What's wrong?" His tone shifted down.

"Everything's all right." I hated that I lied.

"Is it the boys?... Tell me." His voice was flat and to the point.

"The boys are fine." I hesitated trying to compose my words. "I saw Neal tonight."

"Neal Sullivan, your ex-fiancé?"

"Yes." I had to be careful explaining what happened or Jim would be on the next plane to Philadelphia. "Nothing happened, but there's something I need to tell you. Neal's different. I thought he was over me... he's not. I'm frightened."

"Don't leave the apartment tonight and catch the first flight home in the morning."

I closed my eyes thinking about Neal's cold, blank stare. "We've got to talk... but not over the phone."

CHAPTER 23

LAURA

I HAD NOTHING BUT TIME TO THINK ABOUT WHAT TO SAY TO Jim on my flight home. Had I overreacted? Neal didn't hurt me nor did he make threats. But the circumstances of yesterday forced the issue. Could it be possible for Neal to want to kill Jim for something I did?

Jim met us as soon as we exited the plane. My heart rate picked up, fluttering like hummingbirds. When the kids saw their daddy, all three raced toward him, little feet pumping up and down. He scooped them up at the same time, giving hugs and kisses.

When he got to me, he put the boys down and wrapped his arms around my waist and gave me a kiss. "I'm glad you're home."

Placing my head on his chest, my arms went around his shoulders and I squeezed. It was more for me than him.

"Let's get the boys home. Then we'll talk. You okay with that?" Jim had a way of staying on top of things concerning the family and that comforted me. He always put us first.

I needed to think rationally before explaining what happened yesterday. It would be difficult because the smell of Neal's liquored breath and his twisted words had shaken me to the core. But—when I thought of him touching my hair—steel hands clawed at my chest. His audacity repulsed me.

How would Jim respond? God help Neal if my husband decided to take matters into his own hands. How could I have been so very wrong about the man I had been engaged to? What blinded me from his hidden character?

After going over every detail of my ordeal with Neal, Jim seemed calm, but the tightness in his jaw told a different story. "I'll call Detective Halpin tomorrow morning." We both agreed, if Dr. Sullivan wasn't a prime suspect, he needed to be.

I didn't know how much longer I could conceal my illusion of being strong and courageous. The attempted murder, the death threat letter, and the confrontation with Neal were taking their toll on me.

When would the madness end? And how?

CHAPTER 24

DETECTIVE HALPIN

Jim called this morning at 9 a.m. with the details of Laura's run-in with Neal Sullivan in Philadelphia.

The itch under my collar warned me to take a close look at this guy. I set a time to visit Dr. Sullivan at his office complex in Philadelphia. I needed to handle this interview carefully. Didn't want him to think this was an interrogation. There were two things I was looking for, an unintended message revealed in the conversation and deceptive body language.

I arrived at his office fifteen minutes early. I intended to give the doctor plenty of opportunity to tell me about the recent encounter with Laura. If he opened up, he probably wasn't trying to hide anything.

I noticed the receptionist was filing and putting the final touches on what appeared to have been a long day. "How may I help you?"

"Detective Sean Halpin to see Dr. Sullivan."

"He's seen his last patient and will be with you shortly." She returned to her filing.

I looked around the waiting room. Pretty much standard office colors, gray and blue. Depressing to me. "I see pictures of Dr. Sullivan and what looks to be in a third world country."

She turned with a proud grin. "Yes, the Doctor takes a yearly visit to Zaire, Africa, for two weeks. He provides free medical services. He's a caring man."

Chalk one up for the good doctor.

Thirty minutes passed. I'd checked out every magazine on the table and every picture on the wall — including the NRA membership plaque posted over the door leading to the exam rooms.

At the hour mark, a nurse opened the door. "Mr. Halpin, Dr. Sullivan will see you now." The hallway walls were dull gray with framed black and white landscapes. The black floor tiles felt about as warm as a broken toaster. A thin stream of light sliced through the crack under his door.

I knocked twice with the knuckle of my index finger and then helped myself to the doorknob.

"Come in, Detective." Neal waited behind a large oak desk. "Please have a seat." Each word was distinct. His wire framed glasses hinted intellect, but his narrow shoulders and small arms exposed a weak, physical body.

I offered my hand, but the doctor took a sip of Laphroaig Scotch instead. A half empty bottle set on his credenza.

I centered a maroon leather chair in front of Dr. Obnoxious and eased into it. "I'm Detective Sean Halpin with… "

He dismissed my introduction with a choppy wave of his hand. "I know who you are. I checked you out. What I don't know is why you set this appointment?"

It took all my will power to keep my cool in front of this pompous twit. "You appear to be a man who gets right to the point, doctor."

He picked up the Scotch with a limp wrist, finished his drink, and eased the glass onto the desk. "That I am. So why don't you do what you came here to do."

"How well do you know Jim Pepperman?" I placed my elbows on the arms of the chair and interlocked my fingers.

He leaned across the desk, resting on his forearms. "Why is that important for you to know?"

I faked a grin so hard it made my cheekbones ache. "Someone tried to kill him."

"Am I a suspect?" His tone was as cool as a spring shower.

"Just trying to gather information."

Neal leaned back and propped his alligator shoes on the corner of the desk. "I met the guy once. I was engaged to his wife."

"Who broke the engagement?"

He let loose a deep breath as if completely bored by the question. "She did."

"How did that make you feel?" Oops! That sounded like I was psycho-analyzing him. Dumb, Halpin. Dumb.

"Laura's a sweet girl, but a little folksy... not my style." His head tilted back. "I was about to break it off myself. It would never have worked."

Sullivan wanted to convince me he had no interest in Laura, but his earlier reaction had already exposed his true feelings.

Even though the guy made me nauseous, it was important to maintain a level of rapport. Treating him with respect and avoiding threatening remarks could drop his resistance. "It seems you did the right thing... letting her step out of the relationship before you had to break the news. The way it worked out, she did the dirty work. Not many handle those situations as well as you did."

Neal held up his glass, a gesture of my being on target.

Self-inflated, egotistical jerk. "I know you and Jim weren't friends, but what I'm trying to do is piece the puzzle together to develop some leads on who would want to kill him."

Dr. Sullivan carefully set his glass down, then locked his hands behind his head.

I had to keep the dialogue going. Sullivan appeared to be an elitist snob, and I had to be careful not to jump to conclusions with his answers.

Neal removed his propped-up feet from his desk and pretended to straighten the paperwork. "Look, Detective Holmgren."

"Halpin." Dipwad, punk. I was on a roll today — all sorts of adjectives to describe the doctor.

Neal snapped a condescending smirk. "It's been a long day, if you've got police questions, get to it. I don't have time for idle chit-chat."

I struggled to keep my composure and control the interview. "Sorry, Doctor, you're right. To be honest, don't know what I'm doing here. People break up all the time. It's rare someone wants to kill the person that broke them up."

The baiting comment was meant to elicit a reaction, but I got nothing. The doctor became as stone-cold as an iceberg.

"Off the subject, driving in today I noticed the wooded areas. Hunting's my hobby." I hated hunting—unless it was guys like Neal. "I saw a couple of deer carcasses on the side of the road. I'm looking for a lease. Got any suggestions?"

Neal rubbed his eyes with the back of his hands. "No, I don't hunt, and no, I don't know anything about deer leases."

He seemed annoyed by my question, but why were the black and white sketches in the hallway drawings of nature scenes—deer, pheasants, running water? The magazines in the waiting area were *Outdoor Life* and *Field and Stream*. Okay—back off Sherlock—there were also subscriptions to *Better Homes and Garden* and *Redbook*. But the National Rifle Association plaque was puzzling.

Could he love guns and hate hunting? Could he be an expert with a hunting rifle? I'd check it out.

I stood, buttoned my sports coat and walked to the door, then turned to face Neal. "Oh, one last thing—when was the last time you saw Laura?"

"I don't know." He shook his head, not in denial, but as if he was unable to remember. He appeared in deep thought. "Don't remember the last time I talked to her."

Interesting. I didn't ask the last time he talked to Laura. I asked the last time he saw her. "I don't expect I'll be back, but in case something comes up, I'll be in contact." I gave him a grin. It wasn't a friendly grin, not even a pleasant one. It was an I'll be back if I need to grin.

Things weren't adding up. The interview left me with too many unanswered questions. Why didn't he tell me about seeing Laura? Why did he show no interest in guns when a NRA plaque hung in his office? The guy was too cool for his own britches.

Most criminals were black water pits of narcissism, only concerned with themselves. Neal fit that narrative.

It was dark when I left Dr. Sullivan's office. Most of the building appeared empty. After a brief stop in the men's room, I descended the three flights of stairs to the bottom level. I heard the door to the parking garage slam ahead of me, but didn't see the person. My instincts were kicking me in the gut, warning me. I learned a long time ago to pay attention to such things.

I unbuttoned my coat, making easy access to the Glock in my shoulder harness. Keeping my eyes on the metal door, I slowly walked down the concrete steps, my back against the rail next to the building. Each *tap, tap, tap* of my leather soles on the dirty, gray planks sounded like hollow echoes in a city morgue.

Reaching the bottom of the stairs, I slowly opened the door. The garage was dark except for one dim light in the middle of the complex. The dingy-yellow globe provided enough light to make it eerie, like a scene in a Stephen King novel.

I was parked by a steel pillar some forty feet ahead. The only sounds were a car droning by on the street above me and my heart beating in my ears. The smell of musty stale water caught my attention.

I was halfway to my vehicle when someone revved the engine of their car. The noise was so loud I could feel the shock waves pound against my chest. I looked, but saw nothing, pausing for what seemed an eternity.

The gurgling engine gulped gasoline. Bright, bluish white lights blinded me as the car burned rubber and blasted out of the darkness.

I ran faster than I dreamed possible and dove behind a steel buttress. The car missed me by inches. The smell of burned fuel and the haze of carbon smoke billowed over me. I stood to get a look at the car and, maybe get a license number, but all I saw were tail lights as it exited the garage and sped around the corner.

CHAPTER 25

JIM

THE SMELL OF FRESHLY BREWED COFFEE WEAVED ITS WAY FROM the kitchen upstairs to the bedroom. The aroma of cinnamon-laced oatmeal, the old-fashioned oats Mom used to make, enticed me to finish shaving and take part in my favorite meal of the day.

It would be another half-hour before the boys stirred. Laura and I had the opportunity for quiet time. She was a morning person who never woke in a foul mood, and she set the tempo for my work day. I didn't know what I would do without her. Laura was the foundation of this family, and I was fortunate God blessed me with such a wife.

I entered the kitchen. Laura had her back to me as she removed hot buttered toast from the oven. Her brown hair loosely rolled in a bun on the back of her head reminded me of a little granny — but I wouldn't tell her that. Her red-and-white striped robe reminded me of a candy cane. Cute, really cute.

I wrapped my arms around her waist, and pulled her close to me. "Good morning."

She wiped her hands on a dish towel, then slapped it onto the counter. "You ready for coffee?" Her voice was straight-lined, no emotion.

I eased into the kitchen chair. "What's going on?"

"Last night you talked in your sleep again." Laura set a cup of coffee in front of me and some of it spilled. She pulled on the ties to her robe. Her blank hurt stare needed no explanation "It's the same words over and over. 'No, no, I didn't do it. It wasn't me.' You were flailing your arms and legs. This time it was worse."

Her hands began to shake as tears gathered. "What's happened to you? Why aren't you telling me what's going on?"

I played with the coffee cup, knowing I was going to lie. "Laura, I don't remember the dreams. I don't remember saying the words."

The dreams were of the man in the Minnesota alley. He was dead and the police were interrogating me. In my dreams I was going to prison. My family hated me. I'd lost everything. "What do you want me to say? Do you want me to make up something?" My words were detestable and sarcastic. She didn't deserve that.

Her lips curled down. "I. Want. You. To. Tell. Me. The. Truth. No one can have the same dream, say the same words, and not be reliving something."

This was ripping me apart. I wanted to tell her about the night in Minnesota. I wanted to confide in her. But I couldn't. It would destroy her.

Laura's lips quivered, and she walked out of the kitchen.

The day Dad died had been a low point in my life, but it was nothing compared to what I was doing to Laura. I'd betrayed the love of my life. She'd trusted me, but that trust was evaporating, and there was nothing I could do about it. The shooting and my dreams were straining our marriage. The Minnesota incident could end it.

CHAPTER 26

LAURA

I left the kitchen, my steps heavy and awkward as I climbed the staircase to the triplets' room. I eased open the door and sat in the recliner opposite the boys. Three tiny beds. Three big bundles of love. How peaceful their slumber. To look at them made the world seem innocent — pure and clean. If only our lives were as simple and honest as the sleep of our children.

Why was my life, my safe, glorious life, crumbling around me? What had changed? I didn't know Jim anymore. Had he always been secretive and I hadn't noticed? Was there a private lie he'd been living? Was there someone else?

I pulled my knees to my chest and wrapped my arms around my shoulders. Stop it. I had to get hold of myself. Jim was the best thing that ever happened to me.

So what was wrong with me? If someone tried to kill me, Jim wouldn't be suspicious of my past. How could I ever doubt him? If I didn't trust him now, how could our marriage survive?

I had to put things in perspective. Jim wasn't the kind of person to make enemies, let alone the kind of enemies who'd want to kill him.

Neal Sullivan, that creepy bastard. Was he behind all this? Was I the reason Jim was being threatened?

I'd given in to fear long enough. I wasn't going to live my life as a helpless, wimpy victim. I was going to fight back. I wouldn't let anything separate this family. I wouldn't succumb to the threats.

My thoughts were interrupted by the phone. I'd heard Jim get in the shower so I walked down the hall to our bedroom and answered. "Hello."

"Laura." A low, raspy, altered voice spoke. "The time is coming. It's oh so near. I'm getting my revenge. That's absolutely clear. Jim's clock is ticking. It's winding down. Soon Laura's face will be wearing a frown."

"Jim," I yelled. Then I heard a click.

CHAPTER 27

JIM

I heard Laura screaming for me, stepped out of the shower, and grabbed a towel. "What is it?"

She rocked on the edge of our bed, shaking her head. "It's... it's him, the man who wants to kill you. He was on the phone."

I sat next to her on the bed, trying to calm her. I placed my hand on her knee. "What did he say?"

She shook her head. "I don't remember... something about your time is near or your time is running out." She grabbed a pillow and squeezed. "I can't handle this."

I paused, wanting to say something reassuring. "This may be the creep's big mistake. Halpin's taping every conversation. He'll be able to trace the call."

"Do you think?" Laura stared at the floor, eyes blank, motionless. "Call Halpin, please."

"I will... I will. The boys are waking up. They need you. I'll call him now."

I had hoped this was all a prank and the creep would get his jollies and stop. But hope was crushing me. Hope was the cruelest thing on earth. My family was caught in the middle. I doubled my fist. The guy was a bone to be chewed.

The phone rang, interrupting my thoughts. My heart rate tripled. I slowly lifted the receiver. "Hello." Nothing. The silence was deafening. "Who is this?"

"It's Detective Halpin. The people monitoring your phone called me."

"Did you get the number and the message?"

"We got the message, but he didn't talk long enough to trace the number."

"That's no good." I grabbed a magazine from the bedside table and chunked it. "What's wrong with you people? You're supposed to be professional."

"Hold on. I know you're upset, but we can only do so much with the technology we have. You didn't let me finish. We were able to get the area code. It's from Pennsylvania."

"Okay... that proves Dr. Sullivan was the caller. Can't you arrest him on suspicion?"

"I can question him further, but an area code with no number is not much help. Let me work on this. Let me do my job."

I took a deep breath and exhaled, thoroughly ticked and frustrated. "You'll keep me informed. Right?"

"Absolutely. It's easy for me to tell you to hang tight. The threats aren't coming my way, but that's exactly what I'm asking you to do. Hang tight."

After hanging up with Halpin, I booked a flight to Philadelphia. Neal Sullivan had crossed the line.

CHAPTER 28

JIM

AMERICAN AIRLINES OFFERED A FLIGHT FROM TULSA TO Philadelphia. I planned to be on it tonight. I rummaged through my closet looking for shirts and slacks. The sounds of the metal hangers screeched on the steel clothes rod.

Laura walked into the bedroom. "What are you doing?"

"I'm going to Philadelphia and whip S.O.B. Sullivan."

Laura touched my back. "I'm just as upset as you are, but what good will it do if you go after Neal? We're not even sure he's the caller."

I turned. "Come on, Laura. Who else could it be? Halpin said the call came from Philadelphia."

Laura forced a smile. "Halpin said the call came from Pennsylvania. You don't know Neal's the caller. You going there to confront him won't solve anything. It could jeopardize the detective's investigation. Do you want to do that?"

I shook my head. "Don't interfere. I have to go."

Laura grasped both my shoulders and squeezed. "You have a family. Don't be a fool."

I jerked loose and moved away from her. "Don't ever, ever talk to me like that. You have no idea what I'm going through."

Her eyes widened. "You're thinking of yourself." She pointed to the door. "You'd better get a grip."

I turned. All three boys were huddled in the doorway.

CHAPTER 29

JIM

I stood, facing my sons. The look in their eyes was as clear as filtered water. I'd never raised my voice to Laura before. I cupped my hands over my face and sat on the floor, crumpled against the closet door. I motioned to the boys.

Nothing.

They were like statues.

Laura sat next to me, arms extended toward the kids. All three bolted to us. We held them tightly against our chests.

She was right. Confronting Neal would solve nothing and could jeopardize Halpin's investigation.

Someone trying to kill me was bad enough on Laura. I had decided to tell her about the Minnesota incident. But how and when? Anxiety hung over me like a cloud of smoke. Living a lie was taking its toll.

Work that day was miserable. I'd hurried out of the house without resolving things with Laura.

That night I walked through the back door and saw her standing in the kitchen. I needed to apologize. "I'm so sorry for talking to you like I did. Please forgive me."

She nodded and smiled, the kind of smile that said things were okay. She wrapped her arms around my neck and kissed me on the cheek, the way she did everyday when I got home from work.

After putting the boys to bed that night, I turned off the television. It was half past ten. The ticking of the grandfather clock echoed in the hallway. I asked Laura to sit beside me on the couch. The smell of vanilla shampoo still lingered on her hair. The hint of Chanel softened the moment.

"Laura, there's something I have to tell you." The adrenaline pumped through me so fast it left a metallic taste in my mouth.

Her eyes locked on mine. "The tone of your voice frightens me. Please, let this moment last awhile. I can't stand hearing bad news, if that's what it is."

I laid my head back on the sofa and closed my eyes, thankful Laura had stopped me from spilling my guts.

CHAPTER 30

DETECTIVE HALPIN

I tapped a pen on my desk. We'd had the guy—if he'd talked another fifteen seconds we could've traced the call.

My gut instinct? Neal Sullivan was the caller. Every fiber in my body screamed he was the one. If I went back to him without a specific reason, he'd cry foul and accuse me of harassment.

Two hours later, I was back at his office. Neal had to think he was part of the solution, and not a suspect. I had to ask questions and pay attention to his body language. "Dr. Sullivan, I don't want to waste your time, but I feel you can help us with the Pepperman case. May I sit down and ask a few questions?"

His upper lip lifted, exposing his whiter-than-white, perfectly-lined teeth. Again, he pointed to the chair across from his desk.

I unbuttoned my coat and sat in the chair. "Laura answered a threatening phone call this morning, and we have to assume it was the person who wants to kill Jim." Neal's initial reaction to this comment was important.

Dr. Sullivan shrugged. "So?"

He didn't seem rattled at all.

"We think the call came from the Philadelphia area. Do you know of anyone who had it in for Jim because of his relationship to Laura... a co-worker of Laura's maybe?"

The good doctor leaned back in his chair and looked up and to the left. "No."

His left eye movement suggested he was reliving the call in his mind. Was he lying?

Right handed people telling the truth would look up and to the right when contemplating a question. I knew Neal was right handed. He drank the Scotch with his right hand last time I was here.

"Are you sure?" I tried again. "It's very important."

He paused and rubbed his nose. "No, I can't think of anyone who knew Laura and had a problem with Jim. Doctors and nurses don't usually socialize. So, how would I know?"

When a person lied, blood rushed to the nose, earlobes, or behind the ear causing the spots to itch.

If I was right and he wasn't telling the truth, my assumptions couldn't be used in a court of law, but the clues could set the building blocks to find the truth. I was on the right track.

Keeping the conversation moving with this egotist was paying off. I wanted to observe him more, but his short, terse answers told me to stop.

He stood, spread his navy blue sports coat, and slipped both hands into his pockets. I couldn't prove it, but I was confident he flipped me the middle finger with both hands. "I've got a meeting, Detective. You'll have to excuse me."

I left the office and got into the elevator.

A hand shot through the closing doors and stopped the motion.

Dr. Sullivan stood facing me. "Detective, wait. I need to tell you something." His tone had shifted from condescending to respectful.

CHAPTER 31

JIM

The boys were finally down for the night, and the house was quiet. When Laura and I had put them to bed, all three bawled as if we were shipping them off to boarding school.

Downstairs in the kitchen, I looked at Laura, ready for some peace. "Let's go out on the back porch. I've got something to ask you."

Laura pointed to the fridge, looking frail and tired. She was beat down, too. "Want some lemonade?"

I nodded. "Sure."

Outside, we sat next to each other on the wooden swing. The overhead fan hummed a little too loudly, but the breeze felt good. The large glass of cold lemonade hit the spot. "I'm working on a project for building a new hydrocarbon unit at the refinery in Phillips, and it's a real challenge. I was thinking about going out to Osage Hills State Park Saturday morning. Take a tent. Spend the night. Maybe get away from everything. A little solitude might help me work out some rough details. Would that be okay with you?"

Laura stopped sipping her lemonade, looked at me with a scowl that needed no explanation. "And leave me here by myself?" She slammed her feet on the footstool, sloshing her drink.

"I've got the alarm system in place, and I'll ask the police to make frequent drive-bys, but I'd feel better if Brenda and Mike would spend the night over here while I'm gone."

She set her drink on the table and wiped the spilled lemonade off her hand with a napkin. "Okay. I'm so absorbed with the death threats I can't think straight. I know your work is important. I'll give Brenda a call tomorrow."

I placed my arm around her shoulder and squeezed. Every incident in our lives now seemed to set us off. I hated what was going on. Hated what it was doing to us.

Early Saturday morning I loaded the car, hugged the boys, and kissed Laura. When I got to the exit for Osage Hills State Park, I didn't take it. Instead I headed to the airport in Tulsa. I felt guilty about lying, but it had to be done.

Halpin had talked to Neal a second time, and the doctor admitted to seeing Laura in Philadelphia. The situation wasn't just the shooter and me anymore. Now Laura was involved.

That had gone on long enough. Sullivan had to be the one threatening me. I didn't understand why Halpin hadn't figured it out. He even said he thought Dr. Sullivan was lying to him.

I had to keep Halpin and Laura out of the loop. I'd make the doctor confess if I had to beat the truth out of him.

Laura had seen Neal in Philadelphia, but Halpin mentioned he was going back to his home in Chicago. His address wasn't hard to find after I called information.

All sorts of scenarios ran through my mind about encountering Neal. Would he be co-operative or would I have to threaten him? The latter seemed the most obvious. And I was glad. I wanted him to experience fear like Laura had when he'd intimidated her in Philadelphia.

My flight landed at 3:00 p.m. at Chicago Midway. I rented a green four-door Chevy Impala and headed east for the thirty-minute drive to the Hyde Park residential area. The streets were lined with beautiful old trees and manicured lawns. Most of the houses on South Kimbark Street, Dr. Sullivan's street, looked as though they were built in the early 1900's.

Neal lived in a two-story greystone with a basement and a two car detached garage. I got butterflies as I drove by his house. Strangely, it was like a football game before kick-off when I had no idea how things would work out.

His corner-lot house was perfect for surveillance. I could see the front door and the garage pull-in.

It didn't look like anyone was home. The window coverings were open, but no visible activity. Hoped I hadn't picked the wrong day.

I parked half a block away and rolled down the windows. The August day was suffocating and the humidity felt like a blast from an over-heated oven.

My game plan wasn't diplomatic. He'd either get right to the point and fess up, or I'd kick his worthless butt.

By five p. m., there was still no sign of Neal, and I was hungry. A Chicago hot dog sounded good. I'd noticed a drive-in when I came in from the airport. I picked up a dog, fries, and a soft drink, then headed back to my surveillance spot.

The afternoon limped on, and I had a lot of time to think about what might happen. The longer I waited the more my anger built. My head throbbed.

I thought about Laura in Philadelphia with Sullivan trapping her against the door, stroking her hair, and undressing her with his eyes. I slammed my foot into the floorboard and cussed his name. Just saying his name left a bad taste in my mouth. I turned my head and spat out the open window. I could see me gut-punching the little bum and slapping him around. Wouldn't have to use my fist on his baby face to make my point. I'd bloody him up good like the man in the Minnesota alley.

I looked forward to facing down this man.

A black and white pulled up to a stop sign. Didn't want to appear suspicious so I got out of the car and walked a side street. The patrol car kept going. The officer paid no attention to the empty vehicle. But why should he? I was becoming paranoid and had to calm down.

By nine it was full dark. Desperate for a rest room break, I drove back to the hot dog joint, took care of business, and headed back to the house. Just as I turned onto South Kimbark, a vehicle pulled up to Neal's garage. Neal got out, walked up to the back door, and went inside.

I pulled up and parked directly across from the garage. What looked like a kitchen light came on. My heart rate double-timed. Then the living room light flipped on and the little puke sat in a chair next to a window.

What had Laura seen in this guy? It was beyond me.

I got out of the car and walked across the street toward Neal's. A Chevy Camaro, driven by what looked like teenage boys, turned the corner almost running over me. They honked and tossed a few expletives my way. Stupid kids.

The street was dark except for one light on the corner. Miller bugs darted in and out around the lighted globe as though they were playing a game of tag. The sounds of crickets chirping made me feel like they were watching my every move.

I walked to the first step leading to the front door. The butterfly feeling returned to my stomach.

"Jim." I heard a whisper behind me.

Startled, I turned. No one there. Strange.

I took four more steps and reached for the doorbell. I felt a push to my chest so hard I stumbled back. "Remember the man in Minnesota," the voice whispered. Cold air surrounded me.

"Dad?" I trembled.

"Go home." Another soft whisper.

I felt Dad's presence, heard his warning. Turning and almost falling down the steps, I ran to the car. My feet tangled causing me to stumble. The door jammed. I yanked it open, plopped on the seat, sinking low behind the steering wheel.

I tried to control my shaking, then glanced to Neal's house. He was backing out of his driveway, unaware of my presence.

The whole day had been surreal. What I'd planned was not me. If Dad hadn't intervened, Neal could have met the same fate as the bloodied man in the Minnesota alley. Dad saved me from a terrible mistake.

CHAPTER 32

DETECTIVE HALPIN

I walked into my office and checked for messages. My gut told me the death threats were coming from Dr. Sullivan. A couple of things in his interviews didn't add up. The biggest inconsistencies were the NRA plaque in his office and him not telling me about seeing Laura on my first visit.

I wanted to know more about this guy. Birth certificate info said he was born in Bayside, Wisconsin, a small town of about one thousand in the northern part of the state on Lake Superior.

Matt Patters, the chief of police in Bayside, should be able to fill me in on Neal, if Matt had been a long time resident.

I couldn't help but grin when I saw my note pad taped to my desk. I cut loose the transparent binding with my knife. Loved my co-workers. They were like family.

The chief should be back from lunch by now. I allowed for the time change difference. It was two p.m. Wisconsin time. I dialed the number.

"Chief Patters. How may I help you?"

Must be a real small department if the Chief answered his own phone. "This is Detective Sean Halpin with the Newark Police. I was wondering if you could give me information on a Dr. Neal Sullivan."

The Chief smacked what sounded like gum, then answered. "Is he in trouble?"

"No, just trying to get some background information on a case."

"Okay, shoot." I heard the squeak of a chair and Chief Patters' heavy, labored breathing. I pictured a large, rotund man clinging to the receiver with a puffy right hand.

"Have you known Neal a long time?"

"Went to school together. He was one grade behind me. But I haven't seen him in years."

"Tell me what you know about him."

"Smart, but arrogant. Went to college at the University of Wisconsin. Don't know where he got his medical degree."

"Did he get into any trouble in high school?"

"Only one thing serious." He coughed. "When he was about fifteen Neal cornered a young doe in the city park and beat the poor animal with a baseball bat. A deputy came on the scene and had to put the deer down. The town was outraged. I was too. Several boys in my class wanted us to take matters in our own hands. Fortunately, we didn't."

Wow — aggressive behavior. Neal sounded psychotic. "What happened to him?"

"Let me get his file." I heard the sound of a cabinet drawer open and close. "Misdemeanor charges were filed, found guilty, fined $1000.00. The judge made him attend anger management classes."

"Can you speculate why he would attack an innocent animal like that?"

"My opinion... he was an egotistical little runt. Other kids picked on him because he talked down to them, felt he was smarter. Don't know that he had any friends. Guess he took his frustration out on the deer."

"Do you know if he hunted?"

"Detective," his high-pitched laugh sounded like a hyena, "most people in these parts hunt."

"Even Neal?"

"I suppose. Never hunted with him. I didn't care for the guy, but I'll say this. He won the annual Turkey Shoot every year."

A sick feeling washed through my stomach like brine water. Neal lied to me more times than a politician trying to get elected. And on top of that, he was an expert shot. "Does Neal still have family in the area? If so, what can you tell me about them?"

"His dad was a pharmacist."

"You said was a pharmacist. Has his dad retired?"

"Nope. He's dead."

"What about his mom?"

"She's in prison."

"For what?"

"Neal's mom blew his dad's head off with a shotgun while he was sleeping."

"What? Why did she do that?"

"That's the million dollar question. The Sullivan's were the pillars in the community. Strong Christians, active in civic affairs. Everyone liked them. Voted citizens of the year several times. At the trial, all Mrs. Sullivan said was she killed him. No explanation. The town was shocked. Craziest thing I'd ever witnessed."

CHAPTER 33

DETECTIIVE HALPIN

Thoughts of Neal Sullivan surfaced as I paused at the office water fountain a couple of days after my conversation with Chief Patters. Getting into medical school was tough. Adding a misdemeanor to your record could hurt your chances even further, but Neal was a juvenile at the time of the deer incident. I'm sure that played in his favor. But what did that say of his character?

I'd called Officer Rhonda Greatcastle to do some research on Dr. Sullivan. She was the most detailed researcher on staff, and I used her whenever I could. She'd found that Neal graduated from the University of Texas Medical School and interned at Johns Hopkins. Went back to school and became a board certified thoracic surgeon.

But one interesting fact emerged from Greatcastle's research, and she wanted to see me about it.

Officer Greatcastle entered the squad room. Her gait was confident. Another thing I liked. "Have a seat, Rhonda. What do you have?"

She pulled a grey metal chair next to me, the screech so loud I gritted my teeth, and opened the folder. "Neal

Sullivan has an interesting background. In 1974 and 1975, two women, on two separate occasions, filed assault charges against him. But, the charges were dropped."

"Do you know why?"

"Said it was a misunderstanding."

I leaned back in my chair, twirling a Bic pen. It couldn't have been more obvious if it'd been a blinking red light at a train crossing. "He paid them off."

Rhonda gave me a crooked smile. "That'd be my guess."

"Did the women give a reason for the assault?"

Greatcastle flipped through her notes. "Both said it happened when they'd broken up with him."

This guy was turning out to be a nut case, but smart enough to wiggle his way out of messes. None of it looked good for the doctor. Or for Jim or Laura.

CHAPTER 34

JIM

The flight back from Chicago was quick and uneventful. But the near encounter with Neal left me shaken. Dad's warning before I had a chance to confront Neal may have saved me from a fate worse than death. A prison term for assault and battery would have wrecked my family and torn Laura and me apart.

Pulling into our driveway, I felt nauseous. My lying to Laura about the weekend at the state park was already stalking me. She deserved better. She deserved the truth. But telling Laura would have put more stress on her than she could handle.

The boys saw me from the kitchen and ran through the backdoor to greet me. Putting up the camping gear would have to wait.

I bent and prepared for the frontal attack. All three pounded me. The wrestling-tickling match lasted a couple of minutes. "Let's go see Mom. What do you say guys?"

Ronnie stuck his finger in his nose. "Mommy made cookies. Want some Daddy?" The happy moment of seeing their dad vanished. Cookies were at the top of their list.

Laura had her back to me as she lifted the cookie sheet from the oven. "Okay, boys, they have to cool before you can eat one. Go in the living room. I'll bring them to you."

They scampered out. Chuck knocked Leon to the floor and laughed as he stepped over him.

Laura removed the oven mitt, laid it on the counter, and turned to face me. "How was your trip? Get a lot done?" Her voice was flat enough to slide under the door. The look she gave me would melt porcelain.

I sensed there was more to her actions than the words spoken. "It was okay, but I missed you and the kids."

She tilted her head in a not-so-subtle way. "Hmmm… that's interesting. Briscoli from the Phillips refinery called. He said the hydrocarbon unit was finished last month and wanted you to know things were working fine. Cut the B.S. Jim. Tell me where you were." Laura's eyes lasered right into mine.

What she said made my blood jell. "Okay, didn't tell you the truth about the hydrocarbon unit, but I had to get away by myself. What I did was wrong and I apologize."

She rested her back against the oven, took a deep breath, and exhaled. "Don't know why you didn't tell me the truth. I understand the pressure. Just be honest with me. That's all I ask."

An overwhelming feeling of sadness flooded my heart for my continued dishonesty. I went to the kitchen table, pulled out a chair and sat, then nodded. "I'm sorry. Didn't mean to hurt you."

Laura folded the dish towel, placed it on the counter and sat across from me. "Is there anything else I need to know about this weekend?"

"No."

Hurt flashed in her eyes as she pushed from the table and walked out of the kitchen.

What was I doing? I was lying to the one person I should be completely honest with. But I couldn't tell her about the man in Minnesota. I would do anything to keep Laura from finding out the truth about my bad dreams. The man's bloody face and cold dead stare haunted me. And now, I almost did the same thing to Neal. Not telling her about going to Chicago to face Dr. Sullivan was wrong. But what else could I do? I had no choice but to keep my secrets.

That night, exhausted, I still managed to get a good night's sleep for the first time in days. The next morning I woke to Laura and the boys stirring around downstairs. I was usually up before them, but she'd obviously let me sleep in.

I pulled on a pair of workout sweats and an old Pittsburgh T-shirt and headed downstairs. I looked out the living room window and saw a black four-door pull up in front of our house. Two men in dark suits stepped out and headed up the steps.

I met them at the door. "Hello. Can I help you?"

The larger of the two, a strong-looking man with a square jaw and black flat-topped haircut asked, "Are you Jim Pepperman?"

"Yes. What's this about?"

"Would you step outside please?" His voice was deep. He asked a question, but it was a demand, not a request.

I looked back toward the living room hoping Laura and the kids wouldn't see what was going on.

The square-jawed, no-nonsense guy said, "I'm Detective Scott Lytle with the Minneapolis Police Department. You're wanted for murder. Please put your hands behind your back."

My face flushed and my heart pounded so hard I thought it would rupture. "Hold on." I pushed my hands out. "This is a mistake."

Laura opened the front door. "What's going on Jim? Who are these people?"

"Go back inside with the boys."

The detective forced my hands behind my back. I was cuffed and walked to the car.

Laura ran after me and grabbed the arm of the detective. "You can't come here and do this. Turn him loose."

"Laura, go back inside. I'll call you later."

The detectives rammed me into the back seat. As we drove away I turned and saw the boys run out of the house toward the car. "Stop. My boys. I've got to see my boys."

"Jim." Someone was pushing me and yelling. "Jim. You're having a nightmare. Wake up."

I sat up in bed, swinging my arms, barely missing Laura.

She pulled close to me and wrapped her arms around my chest. "It's okay. You're having a bad dream. Everything's all right."

CHAPTER 35

JIM

LAURA MET ME IN THE KITCHEN FOR BREAKFAST. SHE DIDN'T need to say anything about my nightmare last night, her face a doctoral thesis on sadness and mistrust. Her empty eyes held all the evidence I needed of her grief.

"Honey, the Bartlesville Theater Guild is presenting an old vaudeville type show with lots of Roaring Twenties music. I can get reservations. What do you think?"

She shrugged.

Her back was to me as she rinsed a skillet. I watched her as I ate. Our marriage was crumbling because of me, my life morphing into a dark place that left me numb and frightened.

I left for work that day without saying good-bye to the boys. I'd never done that before. All day, guilt dripped from every pore. Was I losing the most precious people in my life? My kids? The woman I loved?

That evening I came home early. I turned onto our street. Laura's vehicle sat in our driveway. No boys were waiting for me in the front yard. The lights were off, but the door was partially open.

Something was wrong.

I parked on the curb, removed the Glock from the glove box, released the safety and ran up the front walk, leaving my car door hanging open. I pushed the front door farther open. The alarm system was turned off. The only sound was the tick, tick, tick of the grandfather clock.

Silence wailed in my ears. Tension ripped my guts.

My breathing was heavy and fast. Checking the living room first, I inched my way up the staircase. I heard a dog bark in the distance.

Beads of sweat broke out on my upper lip. The boys' room was just ahead. I held the gun close to my chest in firing position.

I looked inside — nothing.

The same for our bedroom.

The house was empty. Where could they be? Had someone — had Neal — taken my family? No, please God, not that. Neal could do anything he wanted to me, but if he touched my family, if he —

Pushing the safety lever to the lock position, I hurried downstairs and flipped the light switch in the kitchen.

A manila envelope with my name on it sat propped on the counter. I recognized the black ink handwriting.

I stared and swallowed hard, not wanting to know what was inside. Anxiety oozed from my body so thick I could smell it.

I laid the pistol on the table and reached for the envelope. The flap was unsealed. I slowly removed a letter.

Jim,

I thought I knew you. I gave you my heart, but too many things are coming to light that suggest you held back yours. The nightmares, the death threats, and the lie about the camping trip. I guess I didn't know you at all.

Our new neighbor April Marteen saw you getting off a plane Sunday. I gave you a chance to tell me about your weekend, but you didn't.

I feel like you don't care enough about me to make things right between us. I feel deceived and betrayed. My faith in you is shattered.

The boys and I are moving to Belleville. I'm leaving you. My lawyer will be in touch.

Laura

CHAPTER 36

DETECTIVE HALPIN

Back in my office returning phone calls, I couldn't stop thinking about the Pepperman case. Sullivan's family was knotted up with mental issues. Neal's behavior with Laura seemed psychotic. I had enough unanswered questions to visit with Dr. Sullivan a third time.

I contacted the Chicago Police and told them I believed Neal was a prime suspect in the death threats to Jim Pepperman. They cooperated fully, offering their support if needed and asking to be in the loop on my interrogation.

Sullivan's tone when he agreed to meet me at the Chicago station sounded ticked, but he agreed without hesitation.

The session was going to be an interrogation, not a chit-chat conversation about hunting.

I hated the word interrogation. It stirred emotions and created tension with the suspect, evoking images of verbal abuse, harsh treatment and intimidation. I wanted to use a more persuasive technique, establish a constructive dialogue between the two of us.

I walked in, sat across the table from him. "Dr. Sullivan, I appreciate you meeting with me again. I realize this cubical in a police station is not ideal for you."

He gave me a look that said I could stick it. "Then why did you ask me to come here, Detective?"

"That's a fair question. I thought it might save you some embarrassment with your staff. Just trying to help you out. You've been very cooperative with the Pepperman case."

He leaned back, folded both arms snug against his chest. His eyes focused on mine. "Let's get this over with."

Neal's body language said he didn't believe a word I said. And he was right. Me protecting his image was a crock.

"When I was in your office in Philadelphia, I noticed an NRA plaque on your wall." I narrowed my eyes and scratched my head. "I'm confused. You said you didn't hunt, yet you're a member of a rifle association. I called Chief Matt Patters in Bayside. He said the two of you grew up together. Do you remember him?"

"Of course I remember the pompous blimp." He puffed out his cheeks. "Did he tell you I was a hunter?"

"He said he didn't know, but offered the fact you were an expert rifle shot, the best he'd ever seen. So, were you a hunter?"

"No."

There was a slight hesitation, a little dart of his eyes.

An indication he could be lying. "Were you an expert with a rifle?"

He nodded. "That was the only athletic skill I had."

I placed my right thumb on my lips. "Strange. Most people who belong to the NRA and are good shots like to hunt."

Neal shook his head. "Not me. I don't like killing defenseless animals."

Really? How would he answer my next question? "Then why did you use a baseball bat to nearly beat to death a defenseless doe?"

Neal leaned back in his chair, dropped his head, and closed his eyes, arms limp at his side. It was as though he felt guilty. Then he raised his head, opened his eyes, and managed a weak nod, possibly showing signs of opening up. "I did attack that deer. I wasn't proud of that."

"We've all done things we're not proud of. I'm not judging you, but why would you attack that doe?"

"Dad bought me a .22 when I was nine. I practiced all the time, shooting at bottles, cans, targets. Firing a rifle came natural. I suppose it was good hand-eye coordination. My dad was an avid hunter, but he never took me with him. On my fifteenth birthday, he bought me a Remington Model 700 deer rifle. I was blown out of my mind happy. All I ever wanted to do was please him. I'd tried sports, but was too small and awkward. This was my chance to make him proud. I practiced several weeks shooting the new rifle. I knew if I got my sights on a deer, I could bring it down. One Saturday morning he took me to a deer blind. It was mid-afternoon. A ten-point appeared about one hundred yards from us. I aimed. My hands began to shake, my breathing heavy. I couldn't pull the trigger. Dad whispered, 'Take the shot. Take the shot.' I couldn't kill that beautiful animal. Dad snatched the gun and called me a weak, sniffling coward. Then he backhanded me across my face.

"Once again, I disappointed him. He never said a word to me until we got home. When he looked at me, those eyes were cold and filled with hate. I'll never forget how the corners of his mouth turned down when he said, 'I'm taking the rifle back. Little sissy boys like you don't need a gun.'" Neal placed one hand over his eyes.

I supposed he was trying to hide the shame. Dr. Sullivan exposed a side to his deplorable life. But, I couldn't get side tracked with emotions. "What happened next?"

"I didn't go in the house, too hurt and let down by the events of the day. I walked around the streets of Bayside to stay away from Dad. It was about dusk when I walked by the baseball field and heard the cry of an animal that seemed in distress. A small doe was stuck in a fence. A deer caused my dad to hate me that day. Anger built to a point of rage. I saw a bat someone had left behind. I grabbed it and struck the deer over and over. Blood splattered on my shirt like drops of rain. The ground turned red and bits of flesh and teeth were next to the whimpering body. In shock, I dropped the bat. I ran, ran as fast as I could to get away from the poor animal.

A police car had driven by. The officer saw what I had done.

"The following Monday a policeman came to the house and took me to the police station. I was charged with mutilating an animal without using a legal weapon."

"How did your father react?"

"He didn't mind me attacking the animal, but was furious when he had to pay the fine."

Neal was talking, not seeing me as a detective, but someone who understood him. "I'm going to ask a personal question not related to the Pepperman case directly. Were you physically abused by your father?"

Neal fiddled with his wristwatch band and stared at the wall. His face was a roadmap of hurt, sadness, and shame. He slowly nodded. "But what he did to me was nothing compared to what he did to my mother."

I didn't care for Dr. Sullivan, but no one should have to experience what he dealt with growing up. His arrogant, narcissistic attitude could be a by-product of his environment. People raised in an abusive home often mirrored that behavior.

"Let's move on, Doctor. I only have a few more questions." I stood and adjusted my tie. "Why didn't you tell me about seeing Laura in Philadelphia on my first visit?"

He shook his head. "I don't know. Guess I was ashamed. Every romantic relationship I've had has ended badly."

I leaned over, placing both hands on the table, looking directly into his eyes. "Where were you on July 26th of this year?"

The tip of his tongue rested on his top lip as though he was thinking. "Los Angeles at a medical conference. I was on a panel that discussed surgical procedures for hiatal hernia repair."

Sullivan was tightening the noose around his neck. His battered family life growing up, the Remington Model 700 rifle for his birthday, the same kind of rifle that shot at Jim. If his alibi didn't hold up, I was going full bore after this guy.

CHAPTER 37

JIM

I lumbered down the stairs the morning after I found Laura's note. I needed coffee. Pots of coffee.

My body felt like I had run back-to-back marathons. Sleep didn't happen last night, but when I glanced in the hallway mirror, pillow lines left on my face testified that I'd at least dozed some.

Life without Laura and the boys left a cement barricade inside my chest. My thoughts bounced from anger to hopelessness. Why couldn't she accept that I couldn't tell her everything? I understood why Laura was confused about my life and the problems surrounding us, but I needed her now more than ever.

I poured a cup of coffee, called my office to say I wasn't feeling well, then headed to the back porch and sat on the swing. The morning was still, the leaves barely moving on the trees. Birds chirped. But I wasn't in any mood to be happy.

The boys' football lay against the fence. Laura's favorite cup set on the wicker table, her lipstick print visible on the rim.

Tension built. I pounded my fist into the porch swing. I picked up her china cup and slung it against the brick wall, watching it explode into a trillion tiny slivers. "Why Lord? Why are you allowing this to happen? Her leaving me destroys our family."

I shot out of the swing, paced across the porch, came back and kicked and kicked the wooden slats on the swing until they snapped into splintered shards of kindling. My lungs heaved. My mouth twisted into a scowl. My heart pounded so hard I felt it in my neck.

I closed my eyes and saw a flash of Laura and her beautiful, brown eyes. I could almost feel her soft skin and smell her perfume. It tore me apart.

I needed to call Laura so we could talk. She'd be at her parents' house. If she would focus on what our marriage meant to us, we could work things out.

Walking back into the kitchen, I reached for the phone. My hand shook. Panic gnawed at my gut. What if she didn't want me? What if it was too late to regain her trust? I pulled on the T-shirt sticking to my sweaty chest and dialed the number.

"Hello," Mr. Pomroy answered.

"Brent, it's Jim. May I talk with Laura?"

He paused. "I don't think that's a good idea." He didn't sound angry. That was a good sign.

I ran my hand through my hair. "Please, I need to talk to her."

"Not now. She's too upset. Let her think about what she's doing. Laura's a reasonable person."

Maybe he was right. I didn't want to make things worse by forcing the issue. Laura didn't like to be pressured. I had to be smart and appeal to her logic.

"Okay. Tell Laura I called."

"Yes, I'll do that. Be patient, Jim." His tone was encouraging.

I heard the boys talking in the background. I lowered the receiver. The pain of losing my wife and not being with my sons twisted my mind.

Time crept by. I'd been five days without family. Couldn't sleep. Couldn't eat. My coworkers avoided me. My temperament was worse than a wounded grizzly.

I had called Laura every day. And every day she'd refused to talk to me.

Her note said that our neighbor had seen me at the airport. I had to know what she said to Laura.

April was kneeling in the front yard working in her flowerbed.

"Hey, neighbor, Laura said she talked to you the other day about seeing me at the airport."

She stood and walked over to me. "Larry and I were waiting for my sister to get off the plane. You were on the same flight. I spoke to you, but I guess you didn't hear. We drove down our street and Laura and the boys were out front. I told her we'd just seen you getting off the same plane as my sister."

"Did Laura say anything?"

"She asked where my sister lived, and I told her Chicago."

April took off her gardening gloves and wiped her forehead with the back of her hand. "Jim, is everything okay?"

I turned and walked away without answering. I was digging a hole for myself that I didn't know how to get out of.

The postman pulled in front of our house as I made my way home. He handed me the mail. On top was a plain white envelope addressed to me with red plastic stick-on letters.

I used my index finger to rip open the seal and removed the document.

Your life's in shambles

Too bad my friend.

The clock is ticking

It soon will end.

Because of you

I am a hater.

Bye, bye, Pepperman.

I'll check you later.

CHAPTER 38

DETECTIVE HALPIIN

I pulled into the Newark Police Station parking lot after a too short weekend. My instinct told me Neal Sullivan was guilty, but that wasn't enough to wrap a noose around his neck. My thoughts had been on Sullivan and his alibi for July 26th. The medical conference in Los Angeles would be easy to check out. I'd get Officer Greatcastle to do the search for me.

I got out of my car the same time Rhonda Greatcastle got out of hers. Her hair looked like she had combed it with a spoon. "Good Morning, Rhonda. How was your weekend?"

She moved her briefcase to her left hand, took a last drag off her cigarette, threw it to the ground, and gave it an angry twist with her heel. "Don't ask."

I raised my left hand, palm up. "You broke up with your boyfriend for the umpteenth time."

Her eyes shot so many pitchforks, I almost ducked. She looked down, then up at me, and scrunched her button nose. "That obvious, huh?"

"Hey, I'm a detective. That's why I get the big bucks. I'm good at reading body language. And besides, you and Glenn break-up every other day. The whole department knows the scoop on you and lover boy."

She burst into laughter. "Oh, shove it, Halpin. You only say good morning in that holier-than-thou tone when you want me to do something. What is it?"

"Ah, you're a pretty good detective yourself. Check out Dr. Neal Sullivan and see if he was at medical conference in Los Angeles on July 26th."

Our conversation put us at the elevator. Greatcastle pushed the up button so hard I was sure she broke a fingernail.

I looked down and noticed my shoe was untied. I bent to tie it.

The elevator door opened, but before I could snug the laces, it closed and went up, leaving me behind. I chuckled, finished tying my shoe, and pushed the up arrow.

Greatcastle was a hoot. I liked that girl.

CHAPTER 39

JIM

I EASED THE DEATH THREAT BACK INTO THE ENVELOPE, something inside me exploded in a flash of frustration. "I'm going to kill you, Sullivan."

Air whizzed through my tight teeth as I ran up the sidewalk, bounded up the steps, and burst through the front door. I picked up the phone in the living room and dialed Detective Halpin.

It rang three times before he answered. "Detective Halpin."

"Sullivan sent me another death threat." My open palm slammed the sofa cushion. "I'm going after him."

There was a short pause, and then, "Is this Jim Pepperman?"

"Of course, it is. Who did you think it was?"

"Your voice. It didn't sound like you. How do you know the letter came from Sullivan?"

I sat on the couch and flung a sofa pillow across the room. "Come on, we've gone over this before. I know Sullivan's the one, and so do you. I'm going to kill that S.O.B."

"Okay, so how are you going to do it? Get on a plane, fly to Chicago, confront him and blow his brains out? You just committed murder and told me about it. You'll go to jail for a very long time. Case closed."

I took a deep breath and exhaled. He'd made his point. "What do you want me to do? Prop up my feet and wait for the scum bag to kill me?"

"Overnight the letter to me. I'll call Chief Langdon. You be careful."

I stared out the living room window, every ounce of energy drained from my body. "Okay, detective. It's time we get the putrid sack of dog-barf and finish this case."

"We'll get this guy. I promise. Just don't do anything foolish."

I agreed and hung up the phone. Halpin's words left little hope. My life was being ruined, and there was nothing I could do to stop it.

I'd passed the time driving around Bartlesville that day. It was dark when I pulled into my driveway, walked through the backdoor into the kitchen. I hadn't eaten since breakfast, but the kitchen was a pig sty, the counters filled with empty pizza boxes, Chinese food cartons, and burger sacks. Laura would never let the house look like that. I pulled out a trash bag, stuffed it, then took it out the back door.

The night air was heavy. I flipped on the back porch light and headed to the dumpster. Halfway to the back gate, I heard someone running down the gravel alley.

I bit my lower lip. My heart pounded. It had to be some kid playing around, right?

I set the sack of trash against the wooden plank fence and slowly opened the gate. The streetlight lit the trash receptacles. I picked up the sack, went through the gate, closed it, the rusty hinges creaking in the night air, then walked to the dumpster. Adrenaline spiked through my body. Something wasn't right. I lifted the metal lid to the trash disposal. The thick stench hung like a cloud of smoke. I flung the trash inside the bin and headed back to the house.

The fence gate to my backyard hung open. I knew I'd shut it. The porch and the kitchen lights were off. I speed walked toward the house. My breathing increased. I turned the door knob and pushed. The squeak from the door made me pause.

I'd left my gun in the living room.

I eased through the partially opened door and inched into the kitchen, my steps light. A loud noise startled me. I stumbled and fell to the kitchen floor. Everything went black.

CHAPTER 40

DETECTIVE HALPIN

Officer Greatcastle left a message for me to call her. I fumbled through the Rolodex on my desk looking for her number. As many times as I'd called her, I should've remembered. I dialed the extension.

"Officer Greatcastle."

"Hey, Rhonda, Detective Halpin."

"Well, hello-o-o- detective. How are you today?" Her tone was light and upbeat.

She must have made up with lover boy. "Did you find out where Dr. Neal Sullivan was the weekend surrounding July 26th?"

"At a thoracic surgeons' convention in Los Angeles. He attended the conference on Friday and Saturday, but left early on Sunday. According to the convention coordinator, he was called back to Chicago for an emergency. The event planner was a little peeved because he was supposed to chair a panel on the last day of the convention."

Sunday was unaccounted for. Where did he go? And what did he do? "Okay, Rhonda, thanks for the info."

"Detective, it was a pleasure to help you out."

Was she kidding? She'd never been this kind. The make-up with her guy must have been one heck of a night. "Rhonda, I'll buy you lunch for your efforts."

There was a distinct pause as I heard air rush out of her lungs. "Do you remember the last time you bought my lunch?" It was as though a scowl crept into that happy, cheerful voice.

"No... should I?"

"Let me refresh your memory." Her tone had shifted back to the cantankerous, no-nonsense Greatcastle. "We ate at the Chinese restaurant around the corner from the station. I had the orange chicken. It gave me the granddaddy of all food poisonings. It was so bad my intestines threatened a permanent shutdown. I've never eaten Chinese again."

"Oh yeah. Now I remember. The Health Department shut the place down the day after we ate there. Does that mean you don't want me to take you to lunch? We can go German? Or Italian?"

"You and bad food are synonymous with my digestive system. Need I say more?"

"Hmmm.... Nope, I think I've got it."

I heard a soft chuckle as she hung up the phone. Some people you couldn't help but like.

The next morning I was late getting into the office. I'd spent half the night struggling with the Pepperman case trying to figure out Dr. Neal Sullivan. My instincts still pegged him for sending the death threat letters, but I had zero evidence to prove it.

The coffee pot in the detectives' muster room looked like the bottom of a tar bucket. No thanks, I'd do without.

There was a note on my desk from Officer Greatcastle asking me to call her. I took off my Glock and put it in the desk drawer and dialed Rhonda's extension.

"Officer Greatcastle."

I loosened the knot of my tie and stretched my legs under the desk. "Good morning, sunshine. What's on your mind today?"

"Because you're my favorite detective, I played a hunch and you won't believe what I found out about your Dr. Sullivan."

That got my attention. I pulled my legs under my chair and rested my elbow on the desk. "Let me have it."

"When Dr. Sullivan left the convention in L. A., he didn't book a flight to Chicago. He bought a ticket to New York City."

I swiveled the chair away from my desk. "Now that's interesting."

"Hold on my friend, it gets better. I played another hunch and called his office in Chicago. The receptionist said he sold his practice and is no longer seeing patients."

Sullivan lied about flying back to Chicago. He was no longer practicing medicine. What was going on with this guy? I rubbed my chin with the palm of my hand. "Fantastic work, Greatcastle. I'm taking you out to lunch for the entire month. There's this new Chinese place—"

Click. The line went dead.

CHAPTER 41

DETECTIVE HALPIN

I booked a flight to Chicago, then stopped by Greatcastle's office to ask another favor. She was on the phone in her office. A copy of Newark's *Star Ledger* sports page covered the corner of her desk, the headline—"St. Louis beats the Mets 3-2." It looked like the St. Louis Cardinals could make a run for the 1987 World Series. I liked the Cardinals because of their colorful manager Whitey Herbog. He was famous for his witty quotes. My favorite was *Baseball has been good to me since I quit trying to play it*. You had to love a guy who was self-confident enough to joke about himself.

Rhonda hung up the phone, angled her head, and squinted. Her eyelashes were so fake they looked like crab legs. "What do you want now?"

"For you to call Sullivan's office in Philadelphia and see if you can get a fix on his whereabouts. I'm flying to Chicago this afternoon to see if I can find out why he sold his practice."

She rolled a pencil between her fingers as she stared me down. "You look like a large female ape made you her love slave."

I felt a grin spread across my face from ear to ear. "Shove it, Greatcastle. My ulcers have been acting up and sleep is hard to come by." I walked to her door before I added, "I know a guy with no teeth who just got out of prison and is looking for a date. I gave him your number."

Her mouth flew open, eyes the size of tennis balls. She picked up a paper weight and drew her arm back.

My cue for a hasty exit.

The flight to Chicago left plenty of time to think about how to prove Neal Sullivan's guilt. Something had to surface. Every crime scene left evidence. I just had to find it.

The last threat envelope had been postmarked New York City, just like the second one. His flying to that city from L.A. had to mean something concerning the letters, but what? When I got back to my office I was going to pull out everything we had and go over the threats again until something showed up. I had nothing else to go on.

My first stop after landing was at Neal's old office. If I was lucky, the new doctor may have kept some of Sullivan's staff. The office was located on North Harrison Street, a beautiful modern, architectural building. A glass door on the seventh floor still had his name on it.

"How may I help you?" A pleasant, attractive brunette greeted me.

"Detective Sean Halpin with the Newark Police Department." I showed her my badge. "I'd like to speak with someone who worked with Dr. Sullivan."

The young lady's eyes blinked as though she was shocked that a detective was there. "Ah... ah... Blanche Rivers. Blanche was Dr. Sullivan's head nurse."

I nodded. "Could I talk with her?"

The receptionist sprang out of her chair so fast her headset popped off like a coiled spring.

Why was she so rattled? There was no reason for her reaction. I took a chair in the lobby and waited about five minutes.

A woman in green scrubs came to the lobby and walked over. "I'm Blanche Rivers. I'm sorry but Rachel, the receptionist, forgot your name. All she remembered was that you're a detective."

I stifled a chuckle. "I'm Sean Halpin with the Newark Police Department. I didn't mean to frighten the young lady. I usually don't get that kind of reaction. Do you know why she responded that way?"

"Rachel's blown away by all that's happening, and she's had to answer so many questions about Dr. Sullivan's departure. Would you like to come back to my office?"

"Sure."

We passed several empty exam rooms down the long hallway. She pointed to the kitchenette. "Would you like something to drink?"

"No, but thanks for asking."

Her office was small, a desk and two chairs. Several framed photos that could be her grandchildren hung on the wall facing her desk. Behind it was a wall plaque with a scripture carved in cursive—*I can do all things through Christ who strengthen me.* She walked around her desk, sat, then pointed to a chair. "Please have a seat. How may I help you?"

I sensed she had something to say. "Do you know where I can find Dr. Sullivan?"

Her cold eyes fixed on mine. "May I ask what this is about? Is he in trouble?"

I shrugged. "Just needed to ask him a few questions about a case I'm working on. Do you know why he quit his practice and where I can find him?"

"No to both questions. I received a letter from him asking me to explain to the rest of the staff that he'd sold his business and who bought him out."

"That's it?"

She shifted her weight, maybe feeling a little uneasy, but I sensed Blanche was ticked. "That's it."

It didn't take a bag of tea leaves to read this lady's mind. She was chomping at the bit to spew her guts about Neal Sullivan. She stood, closed the door, and returned to her seat. "Neal Sullivan was an egotistical, narcissistic, manipulating jerk. I was the only head nurse who could tolerate the bum. I worked for him because he promised to set up a retirement fund if I stayed with him. He set up an interest-bearing account and deposited five hundred dollars a month for the last fifteen years. I kept every deposit slip. Fat lot of good that did me. Do you want to guess what's happened to that money?"

I shook my head. "The account was closed and the money withdrawn."

She nodded. "One month ago. I didn't like the guy, but I trusted him. If he did something wrong, I'll do anything I can to help."

I watched a sad flicker in Blanche's eyes. "Why would he leave?"

Her hand trembled. She shook her head as one tear dropped off her cheek. "I went by his house. There was a for sale sign and no one was home."

I stood and wanted to give her a consoling hug. Instead I shook her hand and thanked her.

Neal Sullivan was a mutt, a human being who deserted his humanity. I would find him. You could count on it.

CHAPTER 42

JIM

I woke up sprawled on the kitchen floor surrounded by darkness, feeling like I had a hangover raised to the one hundredth power. A knot the size of a robin's egg protruded on the side of my head. A chair was turned over next to me.

I pushed off the floor and managed to stumble to the light switch. I flipped it on and off. No power. The street light illuminated the living room. I staggered toward the switch next to the hallway door and flipped it. It didn't work either.

I grabbed the emergency flashlight next to the refrigerator, turned it on, and headed to the breaker box in the garage. Something had tripped the circuit. When I reset the switch, light was restored to the living room and kitchen.

My head throbbed, but fortunately there was no gash. I'd tripped on the chair in the kitchen and bumped my head on the counter, I guessed. I felt foolish thinking someone was stalking me, but not foolish enough to not get my Glock. Just in case.

I had no problem sleeping that night. The adrenaline rush and exhaustion had drained me. The next morning I popped a couple of slices of bread into the toaster, poured a glass of orange juice, and sat at the counter.

I had to call Laura and tell her about the death threat. But would she talk to me? I didn't think I could take it if she refused. After eating my last bite of burnt toast and gulping the juice, I headed to the living room and sat on the sofa.

After staring at the phone for what seemed an eternity, I lifted the receiver and dialed the number. One ring, then another, a third ring. "Come on, someone answer."

"Hello." It was Laura.

The sound of that soft, beautiful voice melted me. My body went limp, crushed by the sadness of her not being here. "Laura, it's Jim."

There was a pause. "Jim, please, this isn't a good time." Her tone was gentle, not angry and aggressive when we last talked.

"I have to tell you I received another death threat."

Air pushed through the phone as though someone knocked the breath out of her. "When?"

"Yesterday. I talked to Halpin and overnighted it to him. I'm okay and I'm coming to Belleville."

"No, not a good idea." Her voice was laced with anxiety.

"It's been days since I've seen the boys. You can't keep them from me, and we have to talk. Please Laura, don't shut me out."

"If I let you come, you've got to open up and tell me about your nightmares. Nothing can be settled until you do. Understand? You're going to tell me what's happened to you."

"Fair enough. We'll talk. I just want you and the boys back home where you belong. I'll see you tomorrow if I can book a flight. Tell the kids Daddy's coming." I slowly placed the received on the hook and closed my eyes knowing I could never tell Laura about the dark past.

So what was I going to tell her?

CHAPTER 43

LAURA

THE BOYS AND I HAD BEEN IN BELLEVILLE WITH MY MOM AND dad for a couple of weeks. I missed Jim. The kids asked about him. All three loved being with their daddy, especially at night when he tucked them in and told stories about dragons. Their favorite was *Pete's Dragon*.

Jim's flight was scheduled to land at two this afternoon. I told the triplets and they were bouncing off the walls with excitement. We needed to be together as a family, but how could I stay married if Jim was hiding something from his past?

The trust factor in our marriage was gone. Until he opened up, we couldn't survive. Could things be worked out? That was the sixty-four thousand dollar question. I could accept most anything he'd done, including an affair. The only thing that would be unacceptable was murder. But Jim was no killer.

Mom and Dad knew we needed to talk so they went to an afternoon matinee to give us time alone. I hoped the kids would cooperate.

They wanted to wear their Pittsburgh football jerseys. I put on Jim's favorite perfume, a Chanel he'd given me last Christmas.

The triplets played in the front yard when Jim's rental pulled into the driveway. He stepped out of the car and my heart rate picked up. I felt it pound like a kettle drum. I was anxious, yet apprehensive.

I opened the front door and walked onto the porch. The boys had already grabbed their father around the knees and yanked him to the ground. Ronnie had his arms around his daddy's head. Leon and Chuck trampolined on his chest.

Confusion swirled inside me about our conversation that would come.

Jim's eyes met mine, and he got the boys off of him. "Hey guys, let me talk to Mommy for a moment. We'll get ice cream later. What do you say?"

"Ice cream," Ronnie said. Leon and Chuck pinned their brother to the ground.

Jim stepped toward me and tried to smile. His smile had always been special, the kind that made me feel safe and loved. His smile today was not like that. It was tight and strained. I wondered if he could no longer smile like he used to.

He slowly walked up the steps and extended his arms. I shivered as I placed mine around his waist. It was a quick hug, not like lovers, but a cordial, good-to-see-you hug.

I looked into his eyes because his eyes told everything. They were darting all over the place. I suspected our conversation was not going to end well.

"Laura, you look good. It's great to see you."

His comments seemed fake. "Would you like something to drink? A Coke, maybe?"

"That would be fine. We can sit on the porch and watch the boys."

I went to the kitchen, opened two Cokes, and poured them over ice. As I watched the bubbles settle, I realized Jim was making an effort to normalize our relationship. My stand-off demeanor wasn't fair to him.

Just as I reached the living room, Mom and Dad drove up in front of the house. I pushed open the screen door. "Thought you were going to a movie?"

Dad rested his arm on the gate and gave a disgruntled wave with his right hand. "We wanted to see the old flick *Gone with the Wind*. I guess there are more senior citizens in Belleville than I thought. All the seats were sold out. How about Mom and I take the boys for ice cream? Okay with you Jim?"

"Sure, Brent. Here, I'll give you some money." Jim started to get up and meet him at the gate.

"Keep your seat." Dad waved him off. "My treat."

The boys were out the fence gate and into the car before Jim could get his wallet back into his pocket. Mom and Dad were wonderful grandparents, and they liked Jim.

We watched the car disappear down the street, both of us staring straight ahead. Awkward was an understatement. I prayed Jim would tell me about the nightmares from his past so we could get our lives back in order. The death threats we could fight together.

I was nervous to the point my hand shook when I lifted the Coke glass to my lips. I made a cutting motion with my eyes toward Jim. "Do you think Halpin can figure out who's sending the threats?"

Jim nodded, his fingers tapping on his glass he set on the coaster. "I do. He seems certain Sullivan's behind this. It's a matter of time before the doctor makes a mistake and Detective Halpin will nab him. He went to Chicago yesterday to do more investigation on Neal."

I reached over and placed my hand on Jim's chair. "We can get through this. We will." I squeezed the chair arm so hard my hand cramped.

Jim turned toward me, the look of his smile, the sparkle in his eyes, lifted my spirits. "Yes, Laura, we won't buckle under this pressure. You and I can do anything together."

It was as though all the ropes that had bound us for the past few weeks were cut away and we were free. Joy spread over my body like a warm shower on a cold day. I jumped out of my chair, grabbed him around the neck, and kissed his cheek. "Yes, Jim Pepperman, we can do anything together. I love you more than I could ever express. You're my family."

Jim got out of his chair, placed his arms around me, and gently held me close to his chest. "Thank you for being my wife. You're the best thing that's ever happened to me?"

I took his hand and lead him inside the house. We kissed, a long passionate kiss. I looked into his eyes. "There's one last thing we need to get in the open — your nightmares. I don't care what's troubling you. We can do anything together, just as you said a moment ago." I placed my hands on his shoulders. "What's ripping you apart?"

He eased away from me. The look on his face, the dejected eyes, and the frozen jaw line indicated he didn't trust me with his dark secret. He rubbed his nose as though it itched. The grin that followed told me his next words would be lies.

"It's nothing. Just old dreams about my football days. You know how much pressure it was for a football team to win. My dreams are about me failing on the field, letting my teammates down."

I closed my eyes, opened them, and ran my fingers through my hair. I walked over and shut the living room door, then sat in Dad's lounge chair. "One day your mother and I were talking right after our marriage. Something came up about your teenage years. She said you had an ornery streak, and whenever you weren't being honest with her you would rub your nose as though it was itching. Over the years, when you've told me little white lies, you always scratched your nose. You just did it again. You're lying about the nightmares."

Jim licked his lips. His eyes burrowed into mine and it frightened me. "I'm not lying. I don't have to tell you about everything that's gone on in my life. You're being too hard on me. Laura, I've loved you since high school, and you had to know. Then one day, out of the blue, you called to say you were marrying that creep Neal Sullivan. You didn't tell me everything. That drove a spike into my heart."

I slammed my hands together. "Why are you bringing up my relationship with Neal? It has nothing to do with your nightmares. I can help you. Just don't shut me out." At that moment I realized something. "You never intended to tell me the truth. You're a liar."

Jim walked over, placed his arms on the chair, locking me in. He moved his face within inches of mine. A rush of anger spilled over his lips. "You have no right to talk to me that way."

I slapped his arms away from the chair. "Get out of my face. Get out of this house."

Jim pushed away from the chair, a broken and sad look on his face.

He stepped back, opened the door, shut it, and left.

CHAPTER 44

JIM

OUT IN LAURA'S PARENTS' DRIVEWAY, I JAMMED THE KEY INTO the ignition, turned it and revved the engine. Without looking I backed onto the street. "If that's the way Laura wants to play, I'm done with her." We'd been married six years and she said the trust had gone from our marriage. I agreed. She didn't trust me. I didn't know her.

I drove to the Newark airport, turned in the rental car, and was on a stand-by list back to Oklahoma. It wasn't my intention to return today, but I couldn't stay, even if it meant not seeing Mom. Thoughts of Laura boiled inside me like a cauldron of bitter water. The flight was delayed which gave me more time to stew over our blow-up. All the love I had for her was draining away. At that moment, it didn't matter.

It was about eight o'clock when my plane landed in Tulsa. By the time I got to my car and pulled onto the highway heading north for the forty-five mile drive to Bartlesville, it was dusk.

I noticed a black sedan in my rearview mirror speeding up behind me. It was too close. What was this nut doing? At the last moment, the driver whipped into the open lane, hit the accelerator, and passed me. I thought about flipping the idiot off but realized that would be just as childish as his reckless driving.

By the time I reached the outskirts of Bartlesville, it was completely dark. In my rearview mirror, a pair of headlights bore down on me. The driver alternated from high beam to low beam. My first thought was that someone was having trouble. I slowed down and pulled over as far as I could and still be on the pavement, but the person driving slowed down directly behind me. My heart rate spiked.

I eased back on the highway, picked up my speed, but kept an eye on the car behind me. The headlights seemed at a safe distance. My heart rate slowed to normal as the city lights of Bartlesville appeared ahead.

That's when the car behind me reappeared, gaining on me, faster and faster. Alternating high beams, then low beams again.

The metallic taste in my mouth was adrenaline rush. I hit the gas pedal so hard the car swerved and almost went off the road. My vehicle skidded on the shoulder of the pavement, scraping like hundreds of fingernails on a blackboard, throwing bits of gravel on the undercarriage.

I tried to gain control. My hands clung to the steering wheel so tight my forearms ached. I slowed to make the large, swinging curve in the road. If I could make it, I'd be out of sight long enough to pull onto the cemetery road.

I made it, thank God, and drove a good hundred yards before I stopped and turned off the lights.

I got out of my car and stood by the trunk. A minute later a car sped by on Highway 75. I couldn't tell if it was the one chasing me. Then the car stopped and pulled over, like some wild animal that lost contact with its prey and was assessing the situation. The vehicle slowly made a u-turn, heading back toward the cemetery road. When the car reached the turn in, it stopped again, then pulled onto the road.

My stomach knotted as though someone had placed me in a torture device and tightened the screws. My heart walloped against my rib cage. My breath jammed in my throat when I heard the roar of the engine racing toward me.

I pushed off the trunk and ran into the darkness, up a sloping hill, down the other side. Running out of breath, I wanted to stop but couldn't. Had to run faster. The next thing I knew I was falling off a cliff, arms and legs wind-milling.

I was going to die.

The fall was maybe ten feet. Lucky me. I'd landed in a dry, sandy creek bed. I stumbled and plastered my body against the cliff wall, trying to catch my breath.

A flashlight beam pierced the night air, swinging back and forth like a World War II search beam.

I felt a bush next to me, big enough to hide under. I drew up in a ball and held my breath. Still. Be still.

The flash light beam bounced off the hill across from me.

What would I do if the person found me? One thing for certain, I'd fight with all I had.

After the light vanished, I waited at least fifteen minutes to make sure whoever had been out there was gone.

I had to take a chance. Slowly and quietly, I stood. The general direction to my car was back to my left. Each step was cautious. I went down a slope, then back up, and peered over the embankment. My car, just ahead about twenty yards, was silhouetted by the city lights.

No one was there.

I was safe.

CHAPTER 45

DETECTIVE HALPIN

I'd worked late in my office at the Newark Police Station on a hot Thursday night. A circle of sweat had soiled the sleeves of my starched, white shirt. The air conditioning on the second floor shut off at eight to save energy. The stooges at City Hall must've thought detectives worked regular hours.

The oscillating fan on my desk overheated and quit. I walked to the window to stretch my legs. Moths swirled around the street lights below some choreographed dance ritual. A lonesome cricket, somewhere in the building, did what crickets do—annoy humans with high pitched squeaks.

The Pepperman case perplexed me. Something was missing. But what? I'd asked Jim if there could be anyone else involved. He was adamant there wasn't at first, but something caused him to pause before he answered. Was Jim hiding something?

Jim was in serious trouble. I needed to find an answer. Thumbing through the death threat letters for the gazillionth time, I studied each word—*the next time you'll find him dead – time's run out – the clock is ticking*. One note caught my attention. Three distinct words latched on like a claw hammer on a rusty nail.

I leaned back in the chair and broke out into a meat market dog's smile. My laughter was so loud the cricket stopped chirping. I stood and slapped the desk with my open hand. "I've got you, you miserable creep. I know who you are. I know where you are."

CHAPTER 46

JIM

It'd been three days since the road rage incident driving home from the Tulsa airport. Could the driver have been some deranged fool or Neal Sullivan?

I'd become edgy to the point of paranoia, and even though Halpin said he contacted the Bartlesville Police Department and asked for police drive-bys, I took no chances. I made sure the doors were locked at night, the alarm system set, and my Glock never left my side.

I spent tonight flipping channels, watching everything, seeing nothing. The emptiness without Laura and the boys was taking its toll. I missed playing with the triplets after work, then Laura and I talking in bed after the boys were snuggled in for the night.

I'd drifted into a light sleep in my lounge chair, watching the nightly news, when a loud bang startled me.

I gasped and reached for my Glock on the end table and released the safety. There was another loud bang—on the TV. The shots came from a rerun of the gangster series, *The Untouchables*.

I relaxed, engaged the safety, and laid the gun back on the end table. A quick glance at my watch read 1:30

a.m. After checking the doors and turning off the lights, I headed upstairs to bed.

Physically, I was tired to the bone, and my knee hurt. The pain was sharp like someone jabbed voodoo needles on both sides. I'd run too much the last couple of days, overworked a worn-out joint. An orthopedic surgeon in Oklahoma City said another operation might have to be done to repair a tear in my meniscus.

After brushing my teeth and taking a quick shower, I plopped into bed and fell asleep, only to wake up thrashing and shouting, swinging both arms. My T-shirt was soaked in sweat, and I could hardly catch my breath.

Another nightmare. I threw back the covers and placed both feet on the floor. This time it wasn't about the man in the Minnesota alley. It was about the doctor I'd seen about repairing my meniscus. It was supposed to be no big deal, just a quick fix. I'd be out of the hospital the same day. But when I woke up in the recovery room, my leg had been amputated from the knee down.

Neal Sullivan stood over me with a bloody scalpel, laughing a hideous, sick laugh.

CHAPTER 47

DETECTIVE HALPIN

The person I believed to be guilty of the crimes against Jim Pepperman was taken into custody at one o'clock. My preparation and focus had to be professional.

There were basically two types of interrogation. One was coercion, the other more subtle. An old cliché said you could catch more flies with honey than vinegar. When it came to getting people to tell the truth, I thought honey had some merit. But the suspect today would be a challenge.

My inclination was to ask too many questions during an interview. Doing that before the interrogation could backfire. I reminded myself to remain unruffled, soft-spoken, and in control. The suspect had to see me as someone who treated him with respect. If he thought I was the enemy, his resistance could stiffen. The soft interrogation techniques would work to my advantage, but he didn't know that.

Before he was questioned again, I had to make sure my facts were accurate and formulate key questions. It was essential to cover the most important issues first. I only had one swing at the ball so I'd better not screw up.

My plan and strategy had to be rock solid. The timeline for the suspect's activities and details of his alibi were key elements. In other words, padlock him tight to his story.

I brought two soft drinks with me to the interrogation room and stood directly across from the man. My focus was to get him to tell the truth without head-butting and added frustration.

"Thank you for coming. I want to ask you more questions this afternoon about the attempted murder of Jim Pepperman and subsequent death threat letters. The first thing I need to do is read you your constitutional rights."

He leaned back in his chair, arms outstretched, and smiled. "Okay. I've got nothing to hide."

"Thanks for being cooperative. You have the right to remain silent. Anything you say can and will be used against you in a court of law. You have the right to speak to an attorney and to have an attorney present during the questioning. If you so desire and cannot afford one, an attorney will be appointed for you without charge before questioning. Do you understand your rights?"

"I understand."

"Do you give up your right to remain silent and talk with me today?"

He nodded, then gave me a sarcastic eye roll.

"If that's a yes, I must have a verbal response."

"Yes."

"Do you give up your right to have an attorney present while we talk this afternoon?"

He yawned. "Yes, sure."

His cockiness was expected. I'd like to punch his clock. "I appreciate your willingness to cooperate. Where were you on the afternoon of July 26, 1987, from three until six o'clock?"

CHAPTER 48

JIM

THE NIGHTMARE LAST NIGHT HAD BROUGHT ME TO MY KNEES. I'd had enough of my life.

I pushed off the bed and slumped-shouldered my way to the bathroom. The sink was littered with bits of facial hair. Tooth paste clung to the side of the porcelain. A flop house wash basin couldn't have been worse. I turned on the water, cupped my hands and splashed it on my face. The shock of the cold against my body forced me to take a deep breath.

I reached for the hand towel, blotted my face, and looked in the mirror. The person who looked back, surely it wasn't me.

The dark blue circles under his eyes reminded me of a dead person. His cheeks were drawn. His skin color was ashen. The red veins crossing the whites of his eyes reminded me of tributaries from the Mississippi River. The term "death warmed over" would've been a compliment.

I looked long and hard at my reflection. At the guy who'd lost all desire to fight. Throwing in the towel had never been part of my DNA.

The phone rang. It rang again. I let it. I couldn't handle any more bad news. On the third ring I slammed the hand towel to the floor, slung open the bathroom door, and raced to the phone. By the time I picked it up, my jaw felt ready to pop. "What?" I screamed into the receiver.

There was a pause on the other end. Then, "Jim, are you okay? This is Chief Langdon."

I sat on the bed, running a hand through my hair, trying to regain some composure. "Sorry, Chief. What can I do for you?"

"Wanted to let you know Halpin is on to something."

Langdon had a bounce in his voice.

"I can't say now, but I thought you could use a little good news."

He had no idea what good news could do for me right then.

CHAPTER 49

DETECTIVE HALPIN

I LEANED AGAINST THE DOOR IN THE INTERROGATION ROOM, arms crossed behind my back, waiting for the suspect to answer my first question. Nerves ping-ponged inside me, threatening to bust my gut. Didn't want to blow the interrogation. This was my one and only chance.

He finally answered. "Sunday, July 26th?" He thought about it a minute, pinching his lower lip together with his thumb and index finger. "I was at the Belleville shooting range, then went to Tiny's Bar across the street and had a few beers with some old Army vets."

"Is there any reason to believe anyone you were with will tell me something different concerning your whereabouts that afternoon?"

"Um… I don't think so."

"Did you fire a shot at Jim Pepperman at Holy Cross Cemetery on the afternoon of July 26th?" I shot the question at him point blank to observe his reaction.

He rested his elbows on the table, then placed both hands over his eyes. "You're nuts if that's what you think…. No way, man."

"That's why we're having this conversation. My objective is to find out what happened. That way we can clear everyone not involved and move on. Before I get into specific questions, I'd like for you to describe in detail your whereabouts on the afternoon of July 26th from three until six o'clock."

"Told you before…" He covered his mouth, muffling his words. "I went to the Belleville shooting range, signed in, shot for about thirty minutes, then went across the street to Tiny's Bar and chewed the fat with some old friends."

"I didn't make myself clear. What I'm most concerned with is where you were on July 26th at four-thirty." You're working yourself into a corner, stupid. Keep it up.

"You're asking me about specific times. It's hard to remember where I was at exactly four-thirty that day. That was a long time ago, man."

"It's extremely important to nail down where you were at that time." I traced my itchy eyebrow with my finger.

He shook his head and threw out his hands, palms up. "At Tiny's Bar—that's where I was."

I reached into a manila folder, pulled out a photo. "Do you know a man by the name of Delton Watts?"

"Sure, he's… one of the vets who goes to Tiny's. We're good friends."

I slid the colored photo showing a group picture in front him, then stepped back against the door. "On the date we're talking about, Mr. Watt's wife had a surprise birthday party for Delton at the bar. I don't see you in the picture."

He looked over the photo, his eyes moving rapidly from left to right. He licked his lips and paused before answering. "I must have gone to the bathroom." His feet and legs bounced, exhibiting signs of deceptive behavior.

"That could have happened, but the rest of your buddies don't remember you being at the bar on that particular Sunday. They remember you at the range, but not the bar. I'm also puzzled by the fact that you never mentioned there was a birthday celebration."

At that point I had very little doubt this man attempted to kill Jim Pepperman, although I had no clear evidence he took a shot at Jim or sent the death threats. He'd lied about his whereabouts on that Sunday afternoon.

It was time to move from interview to interrogation mode. I had to make sure my transition statement covered the best case—worst case scenario.

I pulled the chair away from the table and sat across from him making direct eye contact. "To be honest, I have a great deal of concern. I would like for you to hear me out. When I finish, I'll give you time to respond. Is that fair? Will you agree to this?"

"Huh... do I have a choice?"

"You really don't have an alibi. After you left the shooting range, you never went to Tiny's Bar. I know that for a fact."

His blank stare focused on me.

I drummed my finger on the table. "I'm aware of what you've done with your life. You're getting an education. You give back to the community. If you weren't a caring person, you would never have done these things.

He nodded.

"Your actions tell me it wasn't a character issue causing you to shoot at Pepperman—it was the circumstance you found yourself in." I pulled a yellow pad and pen from a drawer and laid it on the table. "You were thinking about your past emotionally rather than rationally, and I understand that completely. I also understand you're in a tight spot right now. I'm here to work with you so we can make sense of this nightmare. Killing him was a spur-of-the-moment thing. Sometimes people can't take the pressure. Once you made the attempt on Pepperman's life, it snowballed with the death threats.

"In my world, police work, I've seen situations get out of hand, where people honestly don't know a constructive way to handle their problems. I've worked with people from all walks of life—priests, government officials, businessmen—who found themselves in extenuating circumstances. Circumstances that evolved into a horrible situation. But, you know what? Most of those problems were fixable. We need to get everything on the table so we'll know what we're dealing with. This is the only way it will work.

"Here's how I see it. Your twentieth high school reunion came up. It brought back memories of your football team, memories of Jim Pepperman and how you thought he got you kicked off the team, ruining your chances for an athletic scholarship. He dated a girl you liked—took her away from you. These past issues came to a head, and it was more than you could take."

He reached for his soft drink and took a sip.

I did the same with mine.

His body was tense, rigid.

"Here's the good news. No one was killed. No one was seriously hurt. I don't know what sort of punishment is going to be dealt, but I do know your life is not over. We live in a forgiving society. I know you better than you think, and if I understand you, so will others. Sometimes good people do dumb things. You're a good person. You just made a mistake."

He looked at me like I'd beaten his dog with a rubber hose. "I can't believe you're treating me like I'm guilty. I've come in here at your request without a lawyer. And you know why? I have nothing to hide. I'm respected in my community. They know, as you should, I could never attempt to kill someone. Why would I risk throwing away my life for something so foolish?" His pitch high, he raised his hand and made several wild movements.

His actions again indicated deception. I had to sap his power by neutralizing his comments. "You're exactly right. Everyone I talked with about you had nothing but praise. That's why it's so important we resolve this matter. I'm certainly not passing judgment. That's not my job. We just need to figure out why this happened."

The suspect's face turned red and the veins in his neck protruded. He slammed his fist on the table. "You have slandered, trampled, and maligned my character. That's just wrong."

He tried to steer me away from my interrogation. It was important I remained in control of the situation and not mimic his outburst. I took another sip of my Coke. "I know you're upset." I responded in a soft, relaxed tone and tried to be sympathetic. "Please understand that's not my intent. The last thing I want to do is make this harder for you. And you need to understand that your anger is not going to accomplish anything."

Air surged from his lungs, and he snarled like a cornered badger. "No one has ever threatened me with such contempt. It's no wonder police are referred to as pigs. If there's a way to get you removed from your petty little position, I'll find it."

He was not going to throw me off my game. "As I've said, I know how difficult this must be, but the only way to solve your problem is for me to understand what happened and why. That's how we'll resolve this matter."

He took a deep breath as he traced the outline of his eye sockets with his thumb and calmed down once his outburst had accomplished nothing. "I've told you over and over. I had nothing to do with the attempted murder of Pepperman."

I held up both hands, palms out in a non-threatening gesture. "Sir, it's important to realize this sort of thing could happen to anyone. People respond all the time to their emotions. If they would stop to think about what they were doing, they wouldn't do it. Could happen to anyone. I'm not judging you. You didn't kill anyone. No one was hurt. Believe me, this is fixable. I'm just trying to sort things out." I tested the waters with my last statements. If I got no resistance, I knew I would get a confession. I kept him focused on what was happening today instead of a long-term prison sentence.

He looked relieved as he locked his fingers behind his head and leaned back in his chair. "Things got out of hand. All I could think about in Vietnam was getting even with Jim. It was a dumb, silly teenage thing. When

I got home from Nam, I tried to forget him. Then I got the invitation to our class reunion and all those memories were brought back to life. I hated him for what happened."

"Mr. Anderson, I'd like for you to tell me in your own words how things went south." I slid a tablet and pen in front of him. "This takes a lot of courage. You're doing the right thing. It's not the end of the world."

After Phil completed and signed his confession, he looked at me. "How did you know? You had no witnesses, no weapons, nothing... you had nothing."

I paused before answering. "Do you remember what you said to me at the end of our first interview?"

Anderson shook his head. "Don't have a clue."

"You said, 'Check you later, detective.' In one of your death threat notes to Pepperman, you closed with 'Check you later, Jim.'"

"What? You've got to be kidding me. Anyone could make that statement. That doesn't mean anything... doesn't mean I tried to kill Pepperman."

"You're right. I had no convincing evidence you tried to kill Jim Pepperman. I played a hunch." I picked up the tablet and the pen. "But what I do have is your confession."

Before Phil Anderson was handcuffed, I thought of two other questions regarding the case. "Mr. Anderson, how did you know Jim would be at the cemetery?"

He smiled a sleazy, insincere, pathetic smile. I saw the grin of a predator.

"And did you follow Jim from the Tulsa airport to Bartlesville?"

Then he gave me a middle finger salute with his right hand.

In my line of work, there was a fundamental truth. Sometimes good people did stupid things, but this dude wasn't good. My job was to get to the truth and leave the suspect with as much dignity as possible.

Not every interrogation ended successfully. This one did. Jim Pepperman could return to a normal life.

CHAPTER 50

JIM

I REMEMBERED PULLING IN THE PARKING LOT AT WORK THAT morning and turning off the engine, but little else. Chief Langdon's message about good news occupied most of my thoughts through the day. I figured either Langdon or Halpin would call me at home after work. My gut intuition told me something big was breaking, but what?

I turned the corner onto our street, slowed in front of the house, then pulled into the driveway. Normally, the boys waited for me with a football or baseball gloves, but now I waited for a thug who wanted to take me down. My Glock lay on the front seat. I slid it into my pants pocket and walked to the back door.

The phone rang before I got inside. Could it be the good news I waited for? I unlocked the door and hurried to the telephone. On the fifth ring, I grabbed the receiver and placed the Glock on the counter. "Hello."

"Jim, this is Detective Halpin." His voice had a happy ring, and I sensed good news. "We caught the guy."

Numbness spread through me like morphine until I felt like I was floating—relief fighting disbelief. "Excuse me. Did you say you caught Neal Sullivan?"

"I didn't say it was Sullivan." Halpin's words were slow and precise.

My brain crackled. My chest heaved. "Wait a minute. Are you telling me Neal Sullivan's not the one?" I sagged against the counter.

"The shooter was Phil Anderson."

I had a death grip on the phone with my right hand. "Are you sure?"

"Got his confession right here in front of me."

Happiness spiraled from my head to my size thirteens. "Why would Anderson do it? How did you nail him?"

Halpin spent the next twenty minutes telling me everything, ending with what lead to the arrest. Three small words — *check you later*.

A ton of mason bricks had been lifted off my chest. Detective Sean Halpin should be knighted. "Thank you, detective. Thank you so much." Stunned, I slowly lowered the receiver.

It was over. Laughter from the kids next door resonated through the kitchen window reminding me of my boys. In a matter of minutes, life soared from a dark abyss to the top of the Sears Building. The day seemed brighter and the sound of car horns in the distance less angry.

It was Friday night, Laura's and my favorite. We had a standing date without the kids. I wanted to call her. Tell her our nightmare was over, then something inside me clicked like a circuit breaker, and I knew I couldn't. Not yet.

CHAPTER 51

JIM

The nightmare wasn't over. I still didn't know what happened with the man in the Minnesota alley. Not telling Laura about him or the dreams I'd been having caused our problems in the first place. I had to be honest. She and I both deserved the truth. And if I killed him, there was only one thing to do. Turn myself in.

A cold sweat popped out across my neck and back. I could lose everything. My family. My life. Sadness clawed at me like a thousand hands ripping me apart.

I slid into the sofa, my head tilted back, staring at the ceiling. I had to tell Laura. But what would I say? How would she respond? I couldn't bear the thought of her rejection.

Reaching for the phone, I pulled back, hesitant to put my life on the line. I had to call Laura. It was the right thing to do. In one swift move, I picked up the receiver and dialed the number. It rang. And rang. And rang. I felt lightheaded and nervous. Someone needed to answer before my courage evaporated and I chickened out.

"Hello." Laura's dad answered.

"May I speak to Laura?"

"Jim, I'm sorry. She took the boys to the park."

That couldn't be happening. No way could I make this call again. I covered my eyes and slammed both feet on the floor.

"Hold on. I just saw her pull in front of the house." A hollow sound came from the phone like it was placed on a hard surface. The sound of the squeaky front door opening echoed through the line, the same sound I'd heard hundreds of times. I could barely make out him saying, "Jim's on the line."

I waited for what seemed an eternity. The grandfather clock in our hallway ticked, ticked, ticked. What was taking so long? Was she going to talk to me?

"Hello." Her voice came on the line, dead, void of love she'd once had for me.

I forced myself to speak. "I've got good news." My pitch was high, almost yelling.

"What is it?"

"Halpin called and said he caught the guy trying to kill me. It was Phil Anderson."

I heard her gasp. "Did you say Phil Anderson? It wasn't Neal Sullivan?"

"Anderson signed a confession. It's over."

Muffled cries poured from Laura. It was as though the flood gates released. She took a deep breath, then cleared her throat. "Why would Anderson do such a thing? You two had issues, but that was kid's stuff."

"I asked the same question. Halpin said he would fill me in."

"Are you…" she sniffed, "coming here?"

"Do you want me to?" I didn't wait for her answer. "There's one other thing I've got to do." I swallowed hard. "Please sit if you're standing."

I heard what sounded like a newspaper being picked up. "Okay. What is it?"

"Do you remember the bachelor party I went to for Shannon—one of the engineers I work with?"

"Wasn't it at a dive bar? Some biker place?"

"Something happened that night. It brought up memories of a similar incident that happened when I played for the Steelers. A bully picked on a little guy and humiliated the man."

"Go on."

"Eleven years ago, Pittsburgh lost to the Vikings in Minnesota. Plane trouble caused us to spend the night. I didn't want to be around my teammates after our meal. I went to a bar a couple of blocks from the hotel. I drank too much. A bully, just like the one at the biker bar in Bartlesville, picked on a little guy. I told him to stop. We got into an argument. I knew things were going sour so I left. The man followed me out. He grabbed me from behind and we fought. He was a bloody mess after I finished. The next morning I turned on the TV and the local news reported a man was found dead in an alley." I paused, rubbing my sweaty palm on my leg.

Laura's breathing was heavy and labored. "Why couldn't you tell me about the nightmares?"

Something in her tone made me ache. How could I not have trusted her? "I was afraid you'd leave me. It happened so long ago and I'd forced it out of my mind until the bachelor party. I'm so sorry for lying to you.

You have to understand, you and the boys are my life. I would die without my family."

"Did you say the man followed you out and started the fight?"

"Yes."

"If you did kill the man, it sounds like self-defense. Why didn't you go to the police the next day and tell them what happened?"

"I've asked myself that question many times. Fear stopped me."

"What are you going to do now?"

"I'm flying to Minnesota tomorrow and clear up this mess. If I find out I did kill the guy, I'm turning myself in."

All I could hear was Laura breathing. What would she say next? Was all of this too much? Had I gone too far? "Listen to me. You're not a killer. You're a decent man, a kind man and you have my support one hundred per cent. I'll stand by you no matter what. We'll get through this."

At that moment, I felt relaxed and at peace for the first time since the nightmares started five months ago. No matter what I found out, I had Laura. I had my family. And I could do this. "I'll call when I find out. I love you." I lowered the phone and gazed out the picture window. By tomorrow, I'd be a free man or locked up.

CHAPTER 52

JIM

My flight to Minneapolis landed mid-afternoon. I got a room at the same hotel where I'd stayed with the Steelers eleven years ago. After checking in, I headed to the bar where the fight happened.

As I reached the front of the Irish pub, I had a sense of Dad's presence. "Dad, you were first to know about the man in the alley," I whispered. "Are you with me?"

All I felt was the pounding of my heart thumping against my chest. I heard the buzzing of an old neon light and looked up. I hadn't noticed before, but the name of the lounge was Lucky's. How ironic. This place definitely wasn't lucky for me.

I pushed open the stained-glass door to folk music and the stale stench of cigarette smoke. My knees shook. It took all my strength to keep from turning and running.

A few customers were seated at the long mahogany bar. One gentleman, in the back, sat alone at a table pushed against the wall. A tall, slim bartender, his back to me, faced the cash register counting money.

I leaned on the bar rail and noticed five pictures of men hanging above rows of whiskey bottles. One photo caught my attention. A guy with thick lips and crooked teeth. I swallowed hard. It was Weasel, the guy in the alley.

The bartender turned toward me. "Sorry, sir, I didn't see you walk in." His Irish brogue was heavy. "What will you have?"

"Nothing right now. But can you tell me who that guy is?" I pointed to Weasel. "And why are these pictures up there?"

"Sorry, sir. Don't know the gentlemen's names, but I do know all of them are dead. The owner honors all his regular patrons who've departed. Can't tell you about any of them. I've only worked here six months."

"Hey Big Guy," the lone man at the back interrupted. "Come on back. I knew everyone of those men." He made a pulling motion with his gnarled right hand.

My stomach churned, and my adrenaline spiked. I moved from the bar rail and took a seat across from him.

He wolfed down a beer as though he feared it would get up and run off the table. The baggy-necked fellow pulled a yellow-tinged handkerchief from his back pocket and air-horned his red, bulbous nose. Then he returned the dingy rag to his overalls.

He stuck out his right hand. "Harold Bradford." He shot me a curious eye.

The man just blew his nose on a filthy rag, but I extended my hand anyway. "Jim Pepperman."

The older gentleman angled his head, still checking me out. "Do you know any of those men?"

"The picture hanging closest to the door. He looks familiar."

Harold got the bartender's attention and pointed to his empty mug. "Everybody just called him Weasel because he was so dang ugly." He leaned his head back and laughed, exposing a few missing teeth. His laugh had a queasy sound like his lungs were drowning.

The young bartender plopped a mug of beer in front of Harold who sucked the foam off the frosted glass.

I cleared my throat. "Mr. Bradford, do you know how Weasel died?"

"Weasel was a Viking's fan. One night following a Monday night game, he came into the bar as he always did to celebrate. An hour later, he walked out and never came back. Someone found him dead in the alley just around the corner."

Life drained from my tired body. I thought of Laura and the triplets. The boys having to face the truth their dad was a killer. Laura living in shame, trying to raise our children alone.

How could I have been so stupid? Why hadn't I walked away instead of letting my arrogance take control? I killed a man, for no other reason than my pride. What kind of person was I? No different than Phil Anderson.

"How did Weasel die?" I had to ask the question even if I didn't want to hear the answer.

Harold pointed an arthritic finger at me as though he knew I was the one who killed Weasel. His stare bored a hole through my soul. "A heart attack two years back."

My brain seemed to short circuit. "Did you say two years?"

He pulled a Camel from the pack on the table and stuck it in the corner of his mouth. He lit it, took a drag that went all the way to his feet, then he exhaled. "Yup, two years ago. I went to the funeral. Not many people liked him. Pretty much a jerk. How well did you know him?"

"Not very well. He wasn't a friend." I smiled. I felt it spread from earlobe to earlobe. I extended my hand and stood. "Thank you. You've been a great help. How about me buying you another beer?"

"For what? I didn't do anything."

I nodded. "Oh, yes you did, sir. You most certainly did." I placed a twenty dollar bill in front of Harold and hurried out of the pub, my steps lighter than a Bolshoi dancer.

CHAPTER 53

JIM

I stepped through the revolving door of the hotel and hurried past the registration desk. I was going to get my life back. My wife. My family. My sanity. I couldn't wait to call Laura. A calm spread over me. I'd never expected to be this happy again.

The lobby was jam-packed. I nudged my way into the crowded elevator and pressed the number eight button. It took forever, stopping at every floor. Finally number eight flashed and the door opened.

I caught myself in an almost jog getting to my room and fumbled to put the door key in the slot. Something touched my shoulder, then I heard a whisper.

Son, go get your family and take them home.

Keep reading for an excerpt from Book Two of the
Pepperman Mystery Series

PANIC POINT

PANIC POINT

BOOK TWO-THE PEPPERMAN MYSTERY SERIES

CHAPTER 1

EARL HELMSLY

Morgan lay cuddled in her sleeping bag in our small two-person tent. I turned on my left side, braced on my elbow, and watched my new bride sleep. Her slow, easy breaths brought me peace.

The third day of our honeymoon and marriage was already rounding off my rough, Navy SEAL edges. I reached over and stroked her sculptured cheekbone and jaw line. Her face was a combination of strength and beauty.

"Good morning," she said in a slow, soft voice without opening her steel-blues eyes, the eyes that could hypnotize a Yeti. The corners of her lips peaked upward. The tips of her fingers and the long muscular legs reached from one end of the tent to the other.

I leaned forward and kissed her forehead. "Good morning."

"What are you getting ready to do?" She sat up, wrapping her arms around her pulled-up knees.

I unzipped my sleeping bag and slipped on my cargo pants. Pulling a camo T-shirt over my head, I looked around the tent. "Where are my socks and combat boots?"

She giggled the sort of impish giggle that exuded orneriness. "I told you last night not to leave them outside."

I picked up my pillow and tossed it her way. "A good wife would've brought them inside."

"A thoughtful husband would've thanked me for the reminder."

"Okay, should've listened." I hadn't been married long, but long enough to know I needed to wiggle myself out of this tight spot.

She gave me a wink and an easy nod. "Of course. What are you going to do right now?"

I pulled back the flap of the tent and saw my boots and dirty socks where I left them. "I'm going down to the waterfalls. It's just about a hundred yards from camp. You want to come?"

"No, I'll start breakfast. How long will you be?"

"Thirty minutes. Will that be long enough for you to make yourself beautiful for your fantastic husband?"

She lowered her chin to her chest, and stared up at me, and that stare was an A to Z World Book Encyclopedia stare, implying—don't go there. "Careful big boy. Don't cross that line." A Colgate smile spread across her cheeks. She waved her index finger back and forth.

I had a pretty good idea where she was going with that comment. I gave her a proper military salute. "Yes, Ma'am."

"Oh, Earl, before you go, would you loosen the rope and lower our food from the tree cable? I'll get the salt pork frying and cook some powdered eggs."

The two-person tent didn't allow me to stand so I knelt on both knees, placing my hands on her cheeks, and gave her a good kiss. "You're the best, and you look great when you first wake up."

She gave me a gentle nudge. "Flattery will go a long way."

I pushed through the tent door flap and stood. The day was foggy with a bit of chill in the August air. The beauty of the Great Smoky Mountains of Tennessee was spellbinding. Crows squawked in the distance, and a gentle breeze pushed its way through the tops of yellow birch trees, slowly moving the branches. A squirrel scampered across our campsite, paused and munched on his breakfast, totally oblivious to me.

I turned toward the tent. "Morgan, do you want me to leave the pistol?"

She stuck her head out.

Cute. My heart rate ticked up a notch or two. I knew we belonged together.

"Nope. Won't need it."

I placed my old service handgun, the durable Sig Sauer P226, in my holster and headed toward the falls. The mountain was steep and the forest dense with undergrowth. I had to angle and twist my way through the straight, large birch trees. Morgan's choice for the honeymoon was the perfect spot for me to unwind.

Special Ops missions sucked the happiness out of you. The public rarely heard about our operations. You couldn't know that true evil existed until you saw evidence of people burned alive, were told about children beheaded for playing soccer, or women taken from their homes and never seen again. But I'd be danged if I was going to let those events dominate my life.

When I reached the spectacular falls, the power was overwhelming. The awesome roar of the churning water made me feel insignificant.

I balanced against a rock on one arm, bent and cupped my hand, filled it with the pure, clean, cold water, and splashed it on my face. It took my breath.

I was mesmerized for fifteen or twenty minutes sitting next to the stream. Then a weird feeling someone was watching caused me to shudder, and my adrenalin spiked. I looked around, but saw no one.

The high pitched scream of a cougar far across the mountains rammed hot ice picks of fear into my heart. Panic spread through my body like a kindling fire. Morgan. I had to get back to Morgan.

It started to rain, and I pulled my pistol and raced up the mountain, weaving in and out of the trees. My lungs pounded, desperate for air.

I reached camp. The tent was crumpled. The salt pork smoldered in the pan. And the powdered eggs were scattered next to the fire.

My legs felt like they'd been beaten with a rubber mallet. Paralysis set in, my feet anchored in cement. I lowered the gun to my side and screamed for Morgan over and over.

But she was gone.

PANIC POINT
BOOK TWO-THE PEPPERMAN MYSTERY SERIES

March, 2019

Sign up for my newsletter to get specific information about my books at https://billbriscoe.com

If you don't know how Jim's story started, read *Pepperman's Promise*, prequel to The Pepperman Mystery Series.

ABOUT THE AUTHOR

Bill, a native of the Texas Panhandle, is writing a mystery series based on characters from *Pepperman's Promise*, the prequel to The Pepperman Mystery Series. *Perplexity* is Book One of the series.

Read more about Bill at https://billbriscoe.com/

OTHER BOOKS BY THIS AUTHOR:

Pepperman's Promise
Perplexity
Panic Point
To buy go to https://billbriscoe.com/books

Panic Point audio book
To buy go to https://billbriscoe.com/audio

CONNECT WITH ME ONLINE

https://billbriscoe.com
billbriscoe@billbriscoe.com
www.facebook.com/billdbriscoe

www.twitter.com/BillDBriscoe

If you enjoyed *Perplexity*, I would appreciate it if you would help others enjoy it too. You can recommend it or review it. Reviews can be done at the retailer of your choice.

THE BILL BRISCOE NEWSLETTER

Sign up for my newsletter to receive up-to-date information of books, new releases, and events.

https://billbriscoe.com

FOLLOW MY BLOG

billbriscoe.blogspot.com

TO PURCHASE BOOKS

GO TO HTTPS://BILLBRISCOE.COM/BOOKS

ACKNOWLEDGEMENTS

I want to thank Jodi Thomas, New York Times Best Selling Author, for her encouragement. She always has time for me and makes me feel I can accomplish my dream of becoming a writer. Her influence has started the careers of many successful authors. Exceptional lady.

A special thanks to Morgan Hysinger and Melody Hysinger. You two have been a blessing for sure. I can never repay you for being so generous with your advice on this writing journey.

I would also like to thank the following people who helped bring this book to reality:

Editor: Lori Freeland

Cover and Video Artist: Fiona Jayde, Fiona Jayde Media

Formatting: Tamara Cribley, The Deliberate Page

Website and Computer Support: Michael Gaines

Beta Readers: Sharyn Leiter, Mike Leiter, George Brownlee

Proofreading Team: Brenda Brownlee, Jeff Stenberg, Ora Mae Brownlee, Marjo van Patten

Made in the USA
Columbia, SC
12 November 2023